April's
RAINBOW

CATHRYN HEIN

A South Australian country girl by birth, Cathryn loves nothing more than a rugged rural hero who's as good with his heart as he is with his hands, which is probably why she writes them! Her romances are warm and emotional, and feature themes that don't flinch from the tougher side of life but are often happily tempered by the antics of naughty animals. Her aim is to make you smile, sigh, and perhaps sniffle a little, but most of all feel wonderful.

Cathryn currently lives in New South Wales at the base of the Blue Mountains with her partner of many years, Jim. When she's not writing, she plays golf (ineptly), cooks (well), and in football season barracks (rowdily) for her beloved Sydney Swans AFL team.

Discover more at:

cathrynhein.com

April's RAINBOW
CATHRYN HEIN

Also by Cathryn Hein

Summer and the Groomsman
The Falls
Rocking Horse Hill
Heartland
Heart of the Valley
Promises
The French Prize

For Jim

ONE

The ad appeared in the local paper in April, the month that shared her name. Farm manager wanted. Generous terms. Apply to Quinn's.

Until three months ago, I'd been working for old man McKenna in the job I'd had since I left school, helping him out on the farm that none of his kids had ever wanted but which he couldn't bring himself to sell. Where I wanted to be was home, on Oakvale, but while the family grazing property was fairly large I was the youngest of four boys and there simply wasn't room. Dad hoped I'd get a trade. Mum, being Catholic, hoped I'd join the priesthood. Not a chance of that. Not after Kristy Daley let me kiss her under the footy grandstand one blustery winter afternoon.

So I asked for work at McKenna's and the old boy and I got on well. He grouched, I said bugger-all. I'm one of those big quiet types your mother warns you about, although girls aren't in any danger from me. Kristy notwithstanding, half the time I'm too nervous to speak to them.

I've had girlfriends. Two, to be precise. Both ended up leaving town for bigger and better things. Both times we tried to hold it together but distance never helps any relationship. And my brand of shyness isn't an asset.

Quinn's have been my family's solicitor since Methuselah was a baby, so the week after I saw the ad I called in. Kristy was on the front desk, looking even prettier than she usually did thanks to the glow of a healthy pregnancy. She'd ended up marrying Connor Albrecht, whose family ran the local supermarket, and already had two boys. My guess was she'd keep going until she had a girl, like my mum did.

I stood in front of her with my hat in my hands, rolling the brim like some dumb fool character out of a John Wayne western, barely speaking beyond 'hello', while she nattered away. Finally she stopped trying to coax conversation out of me and instead asked what I was after.

'I wanted to ask about the job.'

Kristy smiled. 'I thought you might.' She tilted her head toward the hall. 'Junior is looking after it. He's free. Go have a chat.'

I nodded my thanks and followed the carpet runner, pausing and taking a deep breath before turning into the open doorway on the right. Junior was leaning back in his chair with his feet on the desk, hands behind his head and his eyes closed.

When he failed to register my presence after a few seconds, I rapped on the door.

Eyes snapped open. The feet slid off the desk. A slightly panicked look fluttered across Junior's face until he clocked who had caught him slacking off.

A grin spread. 'Tristan. How's tricks?'

'Good.'

'Come in. Pull up a chair.'

I did as ordered, shaking hands with him before sitting down. Junior wasn't much older than me, a couple of years at most, which made him around thirty. He'd gone away to Melbourne for uni after school and stayed there until a few years ago, when he'd come home to Rannoch.

Our little town is in the heart of Australia Felix. Which means nothing to most people when you say it, but actually means 'the heart of fortunate Australia'. Major Mitchell, the explorer who coined the phrase, was right. We are blessed here. This part of far western Victoria is lush, fertile, and grows some of the best wool in the country. We have romantic hills, pretty streams and rivers, and reliable rainfall. We also have plenty of erosion thanks to our forebears' enthusiasm for land clearing, but that's another story.

Still, it's a hard place to stay away from if your heart's here. Junior had thought he belonged elsewhere, but one mention from his father of selling up and early retirement and he was back. Apparently, Rannoch without a Quinn as solicitor turned out to be as unthinkable for Junior as it was for the rest of us.

He grinned at me further. 'You're here about the ad.'

I stopped myself from reaching for my hat. 'Yes.'

'You heard Rainbow was sold?'

I nodded, something rustling down in my gut. It was my dream to one day own a property like Rainbow. In two lifetimes I could never have afforded it. There weren't many with the capital or borrowing power who could. Someone had though.

Dad had offered a few times to help me to get started with a small place, even to the point of going guarantor for the bank. I always refused. To everyone's relief I suspect. Money changes things, especially within families. You only had to look at the dust-up that happened between McKenna's kids when he died. They were still squabbling and firing lawyers at one another, while the property – that I'd worked with as much dedication as the old man for the last eleven years – was going to ruin.

It'd happen for me one day, when I'd saved some more. Which was why the ad and its 'generous terms' had me talking to Junior.

'Bought by a woman from Melbourne. An artist.' Junior tossed me a look. 'Interesting type.'

I nodded, a picture forming in my head that wasn't flattering.

'It's not really a manager's job, more a share-farming type arrangement.' Again that look. 'For the right person.'

'What are the qualities of the right person?'

Junior skated his chair back, reached to the shelf behind him and plucked a sheet of paper from a document tray. He rolled back to his desk and propped a pair of glasses onto his nose.

'Usual stuff about pasture and livestock management. You've got all that, no worries.' He rubbed at his chin and I had the feeling Junior was trying to hide a grin. 'Then there are, ah, other things.'

I shifted in my seat and tried not to worry that another job was about to go begging.

'Like what?'

'Patience.'

I said nothing. Everyone knew I had that in droves.

'Kindness.'

I had plenty of that too. Ask anybody.

'Tolerance.' Junior's eyes were fairly twinkling by now. 'And the ability to follow instructions no matter how ridiculous they may seem at the time.'

'Right.' Wasn't much more I could say to that list. Who had those sorts of intangible criteria as job specifications? Artists, obviously.

'Think you fit the bill?'

I shifted again and this time was unable to stop myself reaching for my hat and burying one hand into the crown while the other ran around the soft edge of the brim. I needed this job.

'Yes.'

'Want to put in a formal application?' At my nod Junior grinned. 'I was bloody hoping you would. If you hadn't I was going to ring you anyway. There's no one more suited to it than you.' He stood and reached across to shake my hand again. 'Congratulations.'

'What? I have it?'

'Only person for the job, mate. Give me a week or two to finalise it with the owner and I'll be in touch.'

So that's how I came to April's Rainbow.

If only the rest had proved as easy.

TWO

It was nearing the end of June when April arrived at Rainbow. I'd been on the property six weeks by then, settled into the two-bedroom, simple limestone cottage that came with the job, which sat a couple of paddocks and a long slope down from the main house.

Mostly I'd been getting to know the place. Driving around its hills with my kelpie Holly, inspecting the facilities, checking paddock and rainfall records, and buying sheep. Rainbow was just short of a thousand acres, with the main house a late 1800's single storey bluestone construction with a verandah running all the way round. One of those small but historic houses not uncommon to the area, but renovated to provide modern comforts. Improvements included a three-stand shearing shed, two sets of sheep yards, a couple of silos, and some decaying cattle yards.

As it turned out, Junior's generous terms had proved an understatement. The contract had a few weird clauses that had given me pause for all of two seconds, but pause all the same. In layman's terms, I could run whatever I wanted on my allocation, however I liked, as long as I gave due care for the land and improvements. Sheep, cattle, goats, if I chose. Or nothing. It was up to me because April didn't know the first thing about farming, and she had other things in mind for Rainbow.

For her special part of it, anyway.

The main house was situated off the road on top of one of the property's many hills. Behind it, a small five or so acre paddock sloped down to the highway. Across from there, another hill rose up, topped with a cairn to mark Major Mitchell's trail. A tourist drive looped from the road toward it, ending in a small parking space that offered a sweeping view of the land to the north.

As a local I'd never thought much of it, but a day didn't pass without someone driving up to the cairn for a look and to be battered by the wind that howled across the unprotected cleared hills for miles.

April never called to say she was coming. The first I knew was when I saw a metallic red Range Rover parked in front of the house one morning, every one of its doors open. I didn't know what to expect. Junior hadn't revealed much and I hadn't wanted to ask. The only artist I'd known personally was my mum's cousin Mary, who lived outside of Warrnambool and painted seascapes in thick oils in such a way that it was like the paint formed waves of its own. Two of Mary's paintings hung in the lounge at Oakvale, given as presents in the days before Mary began to command more than the price of a good secondhand ute for her works.

I guess I'd expected someone like her. Older, a

bit crusty and paint splattered. Absent-minded, always looking at people and scenes in a way that made you think they weren't looking at you or the view at all, but something in their mind's eye, as if reality was too boring.

What I got with April was a little of that but much more. So very much more.

There were two parts of the property dedicated as out of bounds for me, unless in an emergency. The house and the small front paddock. Everywhere else on the farm was, for all intents and purposes, mine to do with as I wished. Incredible, certainly eccentric, but I was to learn that was par for the course with April.

I parked outside the fence and stared at the house for a few minutes, expecting her to push open the screen door and come for more things from the car. The house remained quiet, the car abandoned, its doors splayed open like a squashed beetle's wings. I sat for a bit longer, overcome with nerves, until deciding that I had to do something. I collected my hat and jammed it on my head. The day was a fine one for winter, the sun weak but warming and cut by the softest of breezes. A few clouds drifted up high, casting the occasional shadow and causing the light to flicker.

June days didn't come much prettier and it livened my mood. I had another truckload of sheep coming tomorrow and was at last feeling like a real grazier, with my own stock and a future that seemed bright with possibility.

The gate was open. After ordering Holly to stay put I walked through, following the gravel drive toward the Range Rover. At its grill I paused. The duco shone cochineal red, like a bottle of Mum's icing colour, and contrasted with the green lushness of its surrounds. The back lawn was long and capeweed infested. Several times I'd been tempted to run over it with a mower, but defying a contract clause wasn't the way to start off a dream assignment, so I'd left it. It annoyed me though, like I wasn't doing a proper job.

I listened for sounds from the house. The iron roof gave off an occasional ping as the metal expanded in the sun, and I thought I heard something else. A voice, whispering, almost layered, like in a horror film when the filmmaker wants to alert viewers to the approach of hidden, menacing spirits. Even more nervous, I placed my hand on the bonnet of the car and found it was cool.

Nerves gave way to worry. I didn't like this. If she'd been here a while, why wasn't the car closed up? I stepped to the side and scanned the interior. The rear seats were folded down and suitcases packed into the back. On the passenger seat sat a bright orange handbag, its neck gaping open to reveal a purse and a smartphone.

I glanced back at the house. 'Hello?'

No one answered back. I listened for the spirit whispers again but this time only heard the call of a crow.

I moved closer to the house. 'Hello? I'm Tristan. Tristan Blake, the manager.' I swallowed and looked around me, before focusing back on the screen door. The mesh was too dark to make out anything behind it. 'Are you all right?'

After another minute I glanced back at my ute, wondering if I shouldn't drive off and come back later. Maybe she was in the loo or shower, or doing something else private. But the open car doors and handbag had me worried and she could just as well be hurt as occupied. It might not even be Ms Tremayne – as I called her then. I couldn't leave until I knew there was nothing wrong, and Holly had an intent look about her. Clever Kelpie ears pricked, body tense, as though she could feel doubt vibrating in the air.

One of the verandah's red and cream tiles made a scrape when I stepped up. A quick look showed another couple that appeared to sit uneven and in need of recementing. Something for later, when this was resolved.

With a last look back at Holly, I took a deep breath and rapped on the timber frame of the screen door. 'Ms Tremayne?'

Seconds passed. I shuffled a bit and finally succumbed to the urge to check inside, and cupped my hands against the screen, ready to spy.

A noise had me turning to the right. A woman was coming around the side of the house. Her head was down, a vast halo of flowing dark hair falling around her face, lifting gently on the breeze. She wore a long skirt; a sort of patchwork thing in different geometric shapes, vividly coloured. Her cropped jacket was bright emerald and seemed expensive in contrast to her skirt, which appeared home-made. One of those down-filled parkas you bought from brand-name hiking or skiing stores and didn't get much change from three hundred dollars.

Not wanting to frighten her, I cleared my throat.

Ms Tremayne looked up, and for a heartbeat I was lost in the saddest gaze I'd ever seen. Then it was gone, replaced with pure sunshine.

And I knew then that I had found my rainbow's end.

THREE

I removed my hat and stepped off the verandah. I wasn't meant to be in the yard, or near the house. The rest of the farm was my playground and I had no business being here. Except the car, the empty yard and silent house had made me break terms.

I opened my mouth to say something and only managed to wave my hat toward her car.

She glanced at the open doors, frowning, and closed her eyes briefly. 'Yes. Sorry. I was a bit excited and wanted to see the paddock. Left everything as it was. I didn't mean to worry you.'

I cleared my throat, aware of how nervous it made me appear, and felt even more self-conscious because of it.

She cocked her head. 'You must be Mr Blake.'

I nodded, working my way up to speak, but it was impossible with her so pretty and warm-looking, like a colourful tropical butterfly suddenly blown south. And it was strange to be called Mr Blake. No one had ever done that before. I wasn't old enough to be a mister and locals didn't stand a lot on ceremony, not the ones I associated with. The youngest boy of the Blakes was who I was. No room for mister-ing, even if I was the tallest of the lot.

The mister revealed a great deal though, about where I stood in the hierarchy of Rainbow and in April's esteem. I darted another look at the Range Rover, remembered the expensive-looking suitcases, the handbag with its smartphone, and snuck another glance her way. Designer jacket, beautiful hair, long-fingered hands. A million miles out of my social league.

My hands had started their compulsive brim rolling again. I forced them to stop.

She approached, studying me. Not quite as impersonally as Cousin Mary, but like I was something beyond biology, something wondrously curious that appealed deeply to her artist's nature. Her eyes were green. Not murky green but light, with a slightly darker outer ring. Rare and amazing.

'Junior mentioned you were a bit shy.'

I nodded again, convinced my face had developed a baboon's bum flush and, using the same will as I'd used to still my hands, forced myself to speak. 'I saw the car and . . .' I shook my head and began moving quickly up the drive. 'Sorry. Not meant to be here.'

'Mr Blake.'

I halted, a sick feeling in my stomach that I'd screwed up.

She smiled. 'It's all right.'

I glanced at Holly, who was watching me closely, the way she did sheep, assessing the situation, body almost quivering with the need to jump from the tray and canter to my side. She was a good dog, always eager to help.

The dog reminded me of my manners. I might be shy but I was still a Blake. Mum would have clipped my ear if I'd walked away. 'Do you need a hand with anything?'

Again that intense scrutiny. 'You have a nice voice. That's good.' She nodded to herself. 'That's very good.'

I opened my mouth, closed it, unable to fathom a response.

She regarded the car and that strange sadness I'd noticed earlier returned. 'No, I'll be fine, but thank you. That was kind of you to offer.'

I lifted my hat in farewell and strode for the ute, still rolling over 'nice voice' in my mind. Holly leaned her paws on the tray's edge, tail wagging madly. I paused to smooth my hand over her head and murmur to her. Funny how I had no problem talking to dogs, or sheep, or cattle, or any other animal for that matter. It was only people that made my tongue dry out. Holly licked my hand and whined a little.

Suddenly I turned around. April was still by the car watching me. I fondled Holly's ears. 'This is Holly.'

April smiled and raised a hand, twinkling her fingers the way children waved. 'Hello, Holly.'

'She's a working dog but friendly,' I added. It seemed important for April to know. I didn't want her to be frightened if she met up with Holly alone.

'Can I meet her properly?'

I glanced at Holly, straining over the ute, and nodded.

April approached, coloured skirt swirling, thick black curls bouncing around her shoulders, shimmering with light. I wanted to touch that silky hair, wrap a long tress around my fingers and feel it slide away. Even then, on our first meeting, I'd wanted to touch every part of April. Looking back now, the strength of my reaction to her feels a bit over the top and stalkerish, but I owned one of those hearts that could fall in love in an instant and then spend years broken when it all turned sour. Too sensitive for my own good, Mum said. A bloody great sook, according to my brothers. Maybe I was both, but at least the only person I ever hurt was myself.

She held out her curled fingers for Holly to sniff. The dog took her scent and began her welcoming ritual that involved a wag that rippled from the tip of her tail to her head. The sound of April's laughter broke the day in a way that made me think of flowers bursting open in delight at the sun.

She stroked Holly's head, cooing and talking nonsense about what a beautiful dog she was, how her coat glowed the colour of Australia's dry heart, how her ears were special because they could hear the undercurrents of the world. How her eyes were so sharp they saw more than the gods.

They were strange words and fell away as quickly as they'd begun. April's gaze shifted to the horizon, past the rolling hills, to the sky beyond. Her fingers absently stroked but her eyes were glazed, her mind travelling elsewhere. Uncertain, I could do nothing but watch and fret a little, while the air swirled with the soft sounds of country and April's breathing.

A truck along the road broke the spell. She glanced at me and then away, embarrassed. 'Sorry. I get a little distracted sometimes.' She petted Holly one last time and flashed me a quick smile. 'She's a lovely dog.'

I nodded my agreement.

April stepped back and clapped her hands together. 'Right. I'd better get myself organised. Thanks for checking on me.'

'Are you sure you don't need a hand?

'Positive.' She regarded the horizon once more and instinctively I looked over my shoulder to see if I could identify what had caught her attention, but there was nothing. Green paddocks, blue sky, white clouds. A distant stand of remnant forest. The grey steel sheep yards and shearing shed. A crow sweeping past. The usual scenery.

Perhaps she wanted to paint it or something.

'Can I borrow you tomorrow?' she asked suddenly.

I wanted to make a joke, like my middle brother Jeremy would. Wink and say something clever like 'I'm all yours' or 'You can borrow me anytime', but talk like that had never been my go. Half the time I was lucky to get a yes out. Not because I didn't want to talk or was incapable, but because I had a fear of saying the wrong thing. I had every confidence in my livestock and farm management skills, even my mechanical ones when pressed. Talking though, especially to women, was a bugger. Usually it was easier to just 'do'.

So I nodded and tried to make it look confident and normal. The way I wanted her to view me. It seemed to work.

'Will early afternoon be okay?' she replied. 'Say around one or thereabouts?'

The sheep were scheduled for mid-morning. Afternoon would be fine. My gut told me another nod wouldn't be. 'One's fine.'

She breathed out. 'Good. That's good.' The pensiveness left, softening her face. 'I'll meet you here.'

A thought occurred to me. 'Do I need to bring anything?'

'No. Not yet. But later you will.' And with that she hugged herself in secret delight, and skipped back to the house like a child, skirt swinging rainbow ribbons in her wake.

FOUR

It was a Tuesday the day I first saw April dance. A Tuesday afternoon in early winter, with a filthy western district wind blowing and clouds as steel grey and menacing as gunships. And there was April, in that same coloured skirt and bright emerald parka, with her beautiful hair cascading like a black waterfall, arms out, twirling in the centre of the sloping paddock like a magical sprite.

She laughed while she twirled, her head held back, her face to the sky and her mouth open, filling the air with something that sounded to me like pure joy, but that I learned later was something much more complicated, and a hell of a lot sadder.

I'd spent the morning staring like a gobsmacked fool at my sheep. *My sheep*. Merino ewes with soft fine wool and wombs that would one day fill with crossbred lambs. At one point I'd even had a smug little giggle, causing Holly to look at me with her eyebrows raised, which shut me up pretty quick. Giggling at sheep was pathetic, but this felt like I was wrapped in luck. This was the biggest step up in life I'd had and I couldn't remember being happier.

At one I drove over to the main house and

stood by the ute, tickling Holly's belly while I waited for April. A less shy man would have walked up to the house and knocked, but I was still acutely aware of having breached my contract the day before, no matter how okay she'd said it was.

She emerged from the house a few minutes later with a wide welcoming smile that made my heart lurch drunkenly and my skin buzz. Her clothes were the same as the day before except for the elastic-sided workboots on her feet.

She fairly skipped down the gravel drive. An open two-bay shed had been built to the front left of the house as a carport and general junk storage, and the Range Rover was now parked rear-in underneath.

'Hello, Mr Blake.' She held her hand out for Holly to sniff. 'Hello, Holly.'

I nodded. 'Ms Tremayne.'

She slid a look sideways at me, a tiny curl to her mouth. Her lips were shiny with gloss and looked even plumper and prettier than yesterday. I wanted her to ask me to call her April but she just gave me that look and didn't comment. Perhaps she was waiting for me to tell her to call me Tristan. I thought about offering, but the baboon's bum look was already making a reappearance and I decided to save it for another day.

'Shall we walk?' she said.

The main house was surrounded by an inner drystone wall in need of repair, and an outer steel tube and mesh fence to keep stock out of the garden. She followed the edge and I made a mental note to grab a whipper snipper and attack the long grass around the fence before it got even more out of hand. This was outside the restricted area and I'd have no hesitation taking care of it.

'Such glorious country,' she said as we reached the south side of the house's boundary where the front paddock began its slope down to the road. Pausing, she closed her eyes and breathed in deeply. 'You can smell its purity.'

Her cheeks were flushed with cold, her lips parted, the pale skin of her neck pearly. I could have looked at her like that for an hour, she was so beautiful.

To me, that is. My eldest brother Laurie came across April in town one day and described her as looking like a crow in drag. I'd had to shove my clenched fists in my pockets to stop from belting him one, but there was some truth to his description. With her long nose and narrow face April did appear birdlike. I could even concede that her black eyebrows and black hair might give a crow-like impression to some, but crows are sly and mean, and April was open and generous. She had their cleverness though. It shone from her sculptures like they had a beating heart.

She exhaled a long breath. 'This is so perfect.'

I wanted ask what it was perfect for. How could this ordinary bit of dirt and grass be perfect for anything? The slope, while not severe, still made the paddock difficult to renovate, and it was south facing, which meant less sun, especially in the winter. Less sun, less feed, sheep that didn't fatten as well as they could in other paddocks. Definitely not perfect.

'I need to buy some straw. Small bales, dense and very square. It's sharp edges and clean lines that I'm after.' She rested those extraordinary eyes on me. 'Could you source me some?'

I nodded and then cleared my throat. This stupid nodding business was getting tiring, even for me, and I wanted her to see me as decisive and capable. 'Yes, I can do that.'

Even if I couldn't have sourced the straw I would have answered yes to her question. I would have chased the moon for her when she looked at me like that. Besides, having been forewarned, I'd psyched myself for the unusual request part of this job. Not that straw bales were remotely unusual, but I understood that artists thought in different ways to the rest of us.

'How many do you want?'

She scrunched her nose a little. Her index finger flicked an invisible counter as she calculated. Across the other side of the road, a car had pulled up at Major Mitchell's cairn. Two people emerged, hunching against the wind. They stood in front of the cairn with their hands in their pockets, leaning forward to read the brass inscription at the base. Done, they circled the rock pile and stopped back at the front, looking our way.

Spotting us, one raised a hand in acknowledgment. I raised mine in return. April remained caught up in her head, gaze unfocused.

'Fifty-four for the actual design, but I'll need to

allow extra for wastage and experimentation.' She smiled, clearly delighted about something. 'A hundred should cover it. I can source the other materials myself.'

Her gaze returned to the paddock, that secretive smile still twitching her mouth. After a few seconds she headed for the gate. Guessing her intention, I strode ahead and unlatched it for her, holding it open until she passed through, and earning a proper smile in return.

'Thank you, Mr Blake.'

I grinned back, suddenly deciding that there was a certain playfulness to this Mr and Ms business.

Suddenly she darted away from the gate back into the paddock, and my grin turned to panic. Holly belted after her and I followed only to skid to a stop several strides later when April suddenly came to a halt in the middle of the slope, threw her head back, stretched out her arms and began to twirl, laughing at the sky.

Making my heart want to burst with confusion and longing.

FIVE

When I think of artists, I imagine people with slightly vacant stares and the smell of turpentine, or clothes covered in clay and slurry splodges on their cheeks. But art comes in endless forms, and back then, if I was to guess April's choice of media, I would have said it was textiles. With her clothes and worship of the land and sky, natural materials seemed the perfect fit.

A few days after she'd danced in the paddock, I was returning from visiting Dad to borrow some tools. As I went to turn into Rainbow's drive a truck from Miller's came lumbering down the hill. Miller's were our local steel suppliers, and unless April was planning to build a new shed or fence I couldn't see any reason for them being here.

I raised a finger off the steering wheel to acknowledge Darren, the driver, and slipped through behind the truck, driving slowly so I could study the main house. The red Range Rover was back in the drive. In the bay where it had been parked, two pallets of plastic-wrapped goods now occupied the space. I eased to a stop and frowned at a block of equipment I recognised as a welder. Steel and a welder. Perhaps April had someone coming to build her something.

I crawled my ute forward, still perplexed. Movement at the house had me looking up. A man in overalls was emerging from the door. Except it wasn't a man. It was April.

Her wild hair was pulled back from her face and trapped in a thick black plait. The overalls were faded and well-worn. Thick welder's gloves were tucked under her arm and a protective mask dangled from one hand. Spotting me, she grinned and waved.

My foot hit the brake. This wasn't meant to be my business. My job was to run the farm, but with each encounter April caught me more and more in her intriguing web. I couldn't have kept driving if I'd wanted.

She approached the ute, dropping her gear in the tray, and greeted Holly affectionately as I alighted. The dog twisted herself in delight at April's enthusiastic welcome. April glanced at me with happiness and my 'hello' dried up, and was replaced with bashfulness.

'I think Holly likes me, Mr Blake.'

What I really wanted to say was something clever like 'Can't blame her' or 'Holly's always had good taste' – something flattering but fun, to let her know that I thought she was attractive without coming across as creepy. Instead I nodded, which only made her study me closer and intensify my embarrassment.

She kissed Holly on the head, stepped away from the ute, and indicated the shed. 'Today's a special day.'

She looked back at me, green eyes dancing and

reigniting the memory of her twirling in the paddock, an image that had barely been out of my mind. I'd fallen in love with that scene so badly I dreamed it, continually changing it so that somehow it included me, that it was me she danced for. I waited for her to elaborate now, but her gaze had shifted to the horizon again, to that place I couldn't see but desperately wished I could.

The stare went on for an uncomfortable amount of time until April broke it and it was her turn to look embarrassed. 'Sorry. Sometimes I get caught in my imagination.' Her attention shifted to the shed. 'But now it's time to put that imagination to use.' She picked up the gloves and face mask again.

'You can weld?' I blurted.

'Does that surprise you, Mr Blake?'

I took a moment to answer, assessing her tone and expression. She'd sounded mild but perhaps the 'Mr Blake' indicated a tinge of annoyance. I hadn't meant the question to be insulting. I knew women could weld. Women could do pretty much anything as far as I was concerned. I only had to look at my family to know that. Besides, Mum would have given me a good smack around the head for thinking otherwise.

'No.' Short but safe.

'Are you sure about that?'

'Yes.' I paused, forcing my thoughts into something utterable. Short and safe wouldn't do this time. 'Mum says women can do anything they put their minds to, usually better than men.

Something she and Andrea – that's my younger sister – take great pride in proving.'

For some reason it made her laugh. 'Your mum and sister sound like my kind of people.'

'You could meet them.' I cleared my throat, shocked at my own audacity. 'Only if you wanted, I mean.'

'Perhaps one day when they come to visit you at Rainbow.'

I nodded, wondering when that would be. Mum was pretty busy with her volunteer work, and looking after my niece and nephew while Laurie's wife Wendell was at work. Maybe morning tea one day. The kids would love to visit their uncle at his new farm. Or Sunday lunch. Whatever the event, I wanted to make it soon. Mum could talk the hind leg of a horse, and would have April's life story in no time.

Except a big part of me didn't want to share April with anyone.

She waved at the shed. 'I'd better get to work. This is going to take a while.'

'What are you building?'

'Something special, Mr Blake. Something very special.' She smiled and walked off, leaving me to watch the sway of her hips in her overalls.

For the remainder of the week I puzzled over what April was constructing. Each time I passed she was at work, head bent over pieces of steel, sparks flying. Though I slowed and stared, she never looked up, her concentration absolute, and I would drive on, disappointed, Holly at the back of the tray staring longingly behind as well.

The straw delivery was the only time she stopped work. She lay down her tools and followed the truck to the main shed, where I was waiting to help with unloading. April greeted both me and the driver with distraction, her focus on the bales, assessing the density and whipping out a tape measure to check the dimensions. With pursed lips she glanced back at her work area.

A mild panic besieged my chest. What if I'd bought the wrong thing? 'All okay?'

'They're slightly bigger than I calculated.'

The panic worsened. I stopped unloading. Greg, the young guy I'd sourced the straw from, paused too. 'Is that a problem?'

She did that thing again with her finger, ticking off imaginary numbers. 'No. I don't think so.' Suddenly, she smiled. 'They'll be fine. The bigger and brighter the better.'

I didn't understand the brighter reference but it didn't matter. April had smiled and said the bales would be fine. That's all I cared about.

Greg tossed me another bale, a look on his face that I ignored, and hoped April hadn't noticed. I didn't want her hurt.

'Got yourself a weird one there, Tristan,' he said after April had thanked us and headed back to her shed.

'She's fine.'

'What's she making over there, anyway?'

I shrugged. Even if I'd known I wouldn't have told Greg. April might be a bit different but she was far from weird. And it was none of his business.

Or so I thought, but within a fortnight the entire town was talking about April, and I was left battling a mixture of admiration and deep anxiety for this woman who'd granted me a lifelong dream.

SIX

A forward thinking man might have looked up April Tremayne on the internet, but I'd never been comfortable spying. It wasn't that I didn't have curiosity about the world and people. I did. Nature fascinated me, so did people, but my shocking shyness made the latter tricky.

Mum said it came from being the youngest. That as a child I figured out I didn't need to speak because my three older brothers were happy to do it for me. Perhaps there some truth in that, but it still didn't account for the rest of my personality, or the fact that my birth order should have made me the most outgoing of us all. Instead I was the opposite.

I don't know how this happened, I'd just always seemed to be this way. Like my brothers, I played footy and was part of the team, called for the ball and yelled warnings to other players, but the moment we came off the field I'd shut up again. In school, being asked to read aloud or give any sort of presentation proved a trial. I did it, and generally did it well, but the effort was enormous and I'd spend days afterward convinced I'd made a total twit of myself.

It's not as if I was hideous to look at either. My

Blake genes had given me above average height, and like most farm boys I was what you'd describe as strapping. Mum told me in secret once that I was the best looking of her sons, but I think she only said that in an effort to boost my confidence. The girlfriends I'd had seemed proud enough to have me on their arm, and when I looked at myself in the mirror I figured I wasn't bad looking. Dark brown hair and features that seemed in proportion. A straight nose, despite my brother Patrick breaking it when I was thirteen, and a pair of hazel eyes surrounded by dark lashes that my old girlfriend Rachael had called completely unfair on a man, and my other girlfriend Mandy had described as dreamy. I can't really see it myself, nor does it help one scrap with this stupid shyness I suffer.

April didn't seem to mind though. She never prompted me or gave me pitying looks when I didn't speak and had an attack of baboon's bum. She simply carried on with whatever she was doing or gave me one of her artist's stares.

For a while I suffered the delusion that she was capturing a mental image of me for one of her paintings, but April wasn't that kind of artist. It turned out she was a sculptor, one who was once highly lauded before she dropped out of the arts community and disappeared into obscurity. Not that she told me this herself. I had to learn it from the newspaper, four months after her arrival at Rainbow.

Her material of choice was recycled metal, using items as varied as old plough shares, bolts, cogs and cutlery to create fantastical animals and plants. I had no expertise but to me her work was breathtaking. The sculptures seemed to pulse with life and movement, as though they weren't made of metal but something organic and earthy, alive and growing.

Like April herself.

But I didn't know any of this in the early days. All I saw was a woman who danced in paddocks and could weld and had beautiful green eyes and a personality that made my heart feel like a thousand balloons had been tied to it.

It took me a week to work out what she was creating and even then I didn't fully understand, not until the last frame was complete. I sometimes thought she'd made the letters out of order to confound me, but the reality was more likely dictated by practicality. It was only imagination and longing that made me entertain the idea I figured so much in her thoughts.

First, a giant O appeared outside the shed. Then a J, followed lastly by a Y. The structures weren't solid, more like a three-dimensional outline, with fold-out brackets at the back that, when engaged, allowed the letter to stand almost upright. When I first saw the O standing free I'd stressed that April would do herself damage with all that lifting, but the steel was tubular and lightweight, and with the bracket folded in, the O could be rolled easily. The J though required my help to shift, as did the awkwardly shaped Y.

'Joy,' I said to her when we'd lined up the letters in the clear space between April's shed and main machinery shed.

'Yes. Joy.'

I scratched my chin but said nothing. An idea was forming though.

'I'll need more of your help soon,' she said. 'Once I've finished the bales.'

'Sure.'

We both glanced at the sky at the same time as a few wet splatters hit us. The forecast rain had arrived and if the Bureau was right we wouldn't see an end to it for a while. Winter in far western Victoria is cold and wet. That's the nature of our climate, but at those first drops of rain April's face crumpled as though it was the most devastating thing she could have experienced.

'No, no, no!' she cried, arms held out as she faced the sky and twirled, this time not in joy but acute agitation. 'Not now. Not now.'

The rain kept splattering, yet she didn't stop her pleas.

Alarmed, I stepped toward her. 'Ms Tremayne, it's okay. It's just rain. It'll pass.'

She shook her head and I realised that the moisture on her face wasn't all from rain. I didn't understand her distress. I didn't understand her. All I knew was that I wanted to help, to make whatever hurt she suffered go away.

I took her hand, catching her mid-turn. 'April,' I said, letting go to place my hands on her shoulders and bring her around to face me, 'it's okay.'

She regarded me with pooling eyes as though I wasn't there.

I shifted my hand to her back, urging her gently forward. 'Let's get you inside, where it's warm. I'll make you a cup of tea.'

She blinked a couple of times and with a nod, dropped her head in misery, before allowing me to escort her onto the verandah. Only to stay my hand when I went to open the screen door. 'I'm fine now.'

I hesitated. I could tell from her tone I was being dismissed, that I'd crossed a line, but her eyes were red and her mouth trembled and I didn't want to leave her alone with whatever demons had taken residence in her mind.

Her voice firmed. 'Thank you, Mr Blake.'

I stepped away, swallowing, not knowing what to say, not wanting to leave her. Holly had followed us and sat on her haunches nearby, gaze flicking between us.

'I'm sorry,' I said but it wasn't for my actions. I was sorry for whatever troubled her, what made her weld frames of letters that spelled JOY and then made her cry as soon as it rained.

She smiled sadly and opened the screen, then pushed open the heavy timber main door. Warmth gusted out and disappeared in the cold. April slipped inside and, without looking back, clicked the door shut.

I stood on the verandah, throwing looks at Holly, wishing the dog could talk and tell me what to do. In the end I left, but my worried heart stayed behind.

I didn't see April for a couple of days afterward. I looked toward the house and shed often but she stayed locked inside. The frames remained in the centre of the yard, a happy word left empty and forlorn.

Then one day she was there, in the shed, sitting on a straw bale and not in her overalls or skirt but in practical jeans and a polar fleece jumper. I'd noticed the Range Rover gone the previous day and suffered a moment's panic that she'd taken herself away from Rainbow forever, until I realised that she was a normal human with a normal need for groceries.

'Hello, Mr Blake,' she said to me, before greeting Holly with a 'hello, beautiful' that made the Kelpie's tail wag like a mad conductor's baton.

Relief put the shutters on my shyness for once, and I managed a doff of my hat and offered a gentlemanly 'Ms Tremayne' in return. She looked up and I warmed to see the sparkle back in her green eyes. Around her lay great piles of jewel-coloured fabric, fishing line, and a pin cushion studded with thick needles.

On her right, in a neat stack, were several bales stitched into coats of scarlet satin. The suspicion I'd been forming had accounted for the bales but not the satin, and I took a moment to marvel at her cleverness.

'This will take a while,' she said.

Although she hadn't invited me, I took a seat on a bale at the base of the main stack. 'I know how to stitch on a button but . . .' I spread my hands, indicating that they weren't made for sewing. 'I can help lift though.'

'No. You have your own work to do.'

Knowing a dismissal when I heard one, I quickly stood. I'd taken enough liberties as it was, calling her April when she was upset, touching her, expecting her to allow me into the house.

'I'll leave you then.' I made a hand gesture to Holly and the dog reluctantly trotted to my side. I nodded and began striding to my ute, face burning.

'Tristan?'

I took a couple of breaths before turning. She'd called me Tristan.

'Thank you. For the other day. You were very kind.'

She held my gaze, the softness of her look making me sick with love.

'You're welcome.' I breathed in. 'April.'

She smiled and picked up a needle, and began to thread it with fishing line. I continued on my way, the balloons attached to my heart lifting it skyward.

SEVEN

April worked faster than I'd expected, taking fewer than two days to complete covering the bales. Each time I passed she was busy in the shed, but she must have been working in the house in the evenings as well, perhaps using a sewing machine to stitch the satin cases' long sides. Several pie-shaped wedges were now stacked in the coloured pile, with neat round outer rims and sharp points. I guessed these were for the rounded parts of the J and O. There were other odd oblongs as well, the purpose of which I couldn't fathom, but became obvious during set up.

The rain had passed, driven eastward by cold south-westerlies that dug through coats and jeans but at least kept the sky clear, for which I was grateful. Whatever the reasons for April's project, it meant a great deal to her and I didn't want to see her disappointed by more rain.

I used the tractor and trailer to cart the frames to the front paddock, following April's exact directions as to where she wanted them placed. To make the most of the calmer morning, we started early, just past dawn, barely able to see each other's faces for our scarves and woollen beanies.

Except for sturdy jeans, April was back to her bright clothes: red rubber boots, emerald parka, electric blue scarf, and a lurid pink beanie and gloves that seemed to leave colour trails in the rising sun.

The frames were easy to erect. We stood them up in a perfect line that April kept standing aside to sight, the letters casting strange shadows on the grass as daybreak eased to morning. April had asked me the day before to mow a strip across the centre of the paddock and the shorter grass made it easier for us to work.

'I didn't factor that in,' said April, standing further down the paddock and eyeing her work with a frown.

'Factor what in?'

'The slope. The letters are too upright.' She considered for a long moment, then tilted her head to the sky and studied that instead, fists clenching and unclenching. Finally she shook her head, her voice full of despair. 'It won't work this way.'

I regarded the letters, wondering what she meant about it not working. Now that I considered them, the frames *were* too upright. With the bales stacked inside they'd be unstable, liable to tip if the wind got up.

I rubbed my chin. 'We could dig a hollow for the braces. Bury them. That would tilt the frames further back. They'd be more stable that way.'

April stared at me then clapped her hands and did a funny jig. 'Of course! We'll do that.'

Leaving April with her letters and Holly for company, I jogged back to my ute. I had a shovel and mattock at the cottage, where I'd been using them to turn the neglected garden over, ready for spring planting. Gran had promised me seedlings and to help plan the layout. For a farmer I wasn't the world's greatest gardener, but I liked the way home-grown produce tasted like proper food, and in my family a house without a decent garden wasn't complete.

Gran, Mum and Andrea had been out for a sticky-beak during April's self-confinement and I'd had no chance to introduce them. They'd asked about her, of course, but I didn't have much to tell, and I wasn't going to reveal how she'd danced in the paddock, cried in the rain or how often she lost herself in the sky. The frames I gave no explanation for. When asked I simply shrugged, and for once my poor communication skills worked in my favour. Realising I wasn't going to talk they speculated among themselves, relieving me of the burden of having to cover-up.

By then I imagine the entire town had, at some point, had a good gossip about April. She'd bought Rainbow for starters – not a cheap property. She was single, or so it seemed, and wore strange clothes, and she'd employed me via a contract so generous it left people's mouths agape.

Now she was erecting giant letters in her front paddock and filling the frames with satin-covered straw bales.

I laughed to myself as I drove back to the paddock gate. This would really put the cat amongst the pigeons and I couldn't help but admire her for it. April didn't care about other's opinions. She'd never suffered baboon's bum. She danced and cried and felt and built and called me Mr Blake and now Tristan and adored my dog.

No wonder I was crazy about her.

We collapsed the frames and dragged them aside, and I used the mattock to mark out a trench into which the brackets would be buried. Then I started to dig, pausing now and then to erect the O and check the angle. Once April was satisfied, I deepened the trench to the required level along its full length, taking care to keep it as even as possible. Finally, we replaced the frames, standing in front with our hands on our hips and satisfied expressions when the letters inclined perfectly to capture the sun.

'This is better,' said April, before gazing skyward, her green eyes alight. 'Much better.'

I glanced at my watch. We'd been at it for a while, and I was getting hungry and in need of a cup of tea. I slid a sideways look at her, wondering if I hinted whether she'd let me join her in her kitchen for smoko, and then dismissed the idea. I was getting better with her, but that was too bold.

She sensed my scrutiny. 'You've worked hard for me. Thank you.'

'Not finished yet.'

'No.' She smiled. 'Best get on with it then. Unless you want a break?'

Not about to admit to any need for food or sugary tea, I shook my head.

I don't think April had her installation – an arty term I later learned from her – properly worked out. She hadn't calculated how to get the top bales threaded into the frame, or how cumbersome the bales would be to manoeuvre. Without me, construction might have taken the entire day, but I had the tractor and trailer and height and strength, and together we fixed the bales into each letter in the strict order April dictated.

As the morning stretched fully awake, the road began to busy. Locals heading into town, school buses, and livestock trucks heading to the saleyards in Hamilton. Some passed without noticing, a couple honked, but many slowed, peering through windscreens and side windows with amazed expressions or head shakes, and I dreaded the barrage of questions I'd face when I next went to town.

We were both sweating and panting by the time the last bale was secured into the Y. I shifted the tractor up to the gate and strode back down to where April stood, her hands held prayer-like in front of her mouth and tears glistening her eyes.

The sun had risen to its full height now, and the satin bales shone like spectacular jewels, the colours vivid and shifting as the breeze rustled the fabric, and scudding clouds made the light ebb and glow.

Somehow April had made JOY come alive. Steel and fabric and straw made animate, almost quivering. I felt it in my heart when I looked at the letters, the rush coming even stronger when I looked at her. She was crying, but these tears were different from the rainy ones; these were pretty and overflowing with happiness.

'It worked,' she said, turning her face to me in wonder. 'It worked.'

To my shock she took my hand and held it, gripping hard. My heart thumped so violently I briefly thought something was about to burst in it, but it was only the thrill of her touching me.

All too quickly the connection broke, and with a farewell wave April sprinted up the hill. I stood in the paddock, confused and excited, and waited for her to return. After a few minutes I realised she wasn't going to come back. A car engine sounded, cracking my indecision. I jogged toward the gate, reaching it in time to see sun flashing off her car as it sped for the main gate. Concerned, I ran along the fenceline to the other side of the house where I could follow the car. I caught it again as it descended Rainbow's long drive. It braked at the road. No indicators flashed the direction.

Instead of turning, the car proceeded straight ahead, up the tourist track leading to the cairn. April alighted and skipped across the grassy patch that grew in a half moon between the cairn's entry and exit tracks. A quarter of the way down she sat and hugged her knees, her face on her JOY installation.

And there, perched like a pretty bird, she stayed.

EIGHT

By mid-afternoon, April still hadn't moved from her vantage point and I was becoming increasingly worried. I considered ringing Mum or Gran for advice and dismissed the thought. April would be under enough scrutiny thanks to JOY without me making the gossip worse.

Throughout the day, people pulled into the cairn's parking area to take photos of the installation or simply to look and wonder. My stomach clenched in anxiety, I watched a stooped man pick his way through the grass to April. The urge to drive over and protect her made my legs spasm, but to my relief whatever conversation they shared was brief and the stooped man soon moved away.

At three, I filled a thermos with sweetened milky tea and made a couple of ham, cheese and tomato sandwiches, fretting as I buttered and sliced that April might be a vegetarian and be offended. I hoped she wouldn't be. I meant the food and drink to be a kindness, not an offense. She'd been working or sitting now for eight hours. If nothing else, she needed fluid.

I took the quad bike over, the engine loud in the quiet afternoon. Holly was perched on the rear rack, peering around my side to get the full rush of air on her face.

The day was already beginning to chill. I hoped April's coat was thick enough but I'd donned my weathered three-quarter length oilskin in case she needed something heavier to keep out the wind. Even if it wasn't needed she could sit on it. With the thick grass and soil holding moisture from the earlier rain, April had to be half-soaked.

My true goal was to get her back to the house, but my gut told me that would happen only when she was ready. April was a grown woman, answerable to no one but herself. I couldn't force her to do anything. At least ensuring she was comfortable would ease my own conscience.

She threw me a brief smile as I approached and went back to watching JOY.

I removed the oilskin, laid it down beside her and indicated it, determined to get at least a little of my own way. 'You're wet. It's not good for you.'

To my surprise, she shifted across, leaving enough room for me to join her. I'd expected more of a fight. She never said, but I thought she wanted me to share a little bit of her experience. I sat without comment, unscrewed the thermos lid and poured a cup of tea. I passed it over, suffering a surge of feeling when she took a sip and closed her eyes in enjoyment.

'Thanks.'

'I have sandwiches, too.'

She shook her head at those but I unwrapped one anyway and placed it between us.

I turned my attention back to the paddock,

letting her sip her tea while I watched JOY and felt the happiness of it – of her – brighten my world.

Such a simple thing and yet its impact on me, on Rainbow and the landscape, seemed disproportionate. Thanks to the slope and the adjusted angle of the frames, the letters half faced the sky and half faced us. The word seemed incongruous and yet somehow fitting, illuminating the world with its vibrancy.

No matter how weird a person might view JOY, only the most mean-hearted couldn't be moved to smile at it.

'It's like magic,' I said.

'Yes.' Her gaze moved skyward as a contented smile curled her mouth.

'Will you come home soon?'

'When it's dark.'

I nodded. I'd suspected as much. 'I'll come fetch you.'

'I'll be fine, Tristan.'

I picked at a hank of grass. 'You should eat.'

'I will, later. But thank you for thinking of me.'

I wanted to tell her I was always thinking of her, that I would always think of her, but I'd run out of words again. They didn't seem that necessary anyway, not with JOY glowing in front of us in kaleidoscopic colour and our arms almost brushing.

Reluctant to leave, I stayed for close on half an hour, April on one side of me, Holly on the other and JOY shining in front. And when I look back now I wonder if that wasn't the most peaceful half hour of my life.

At sunset I made sure to check that April had come home as promised, releasing a long thankful breath when I saw the Range Rover gone from the cairn and lights on at the main house. I don't know what I would have done if she hadn't moved but there was no way I would have let her stay there all night. Regardless of the consequences, I would have carried her away if necessary. Like I said, I don't talk much but I'm good at doing, especially when I feel strongly about something. And I sure as hell felt strongly about April.

Still do.

I'll never stop. I can't.

She was back the next morning, perched in the same spot even before the sun began to rise. With all the time I'd been spending helping April, things had been let go around the farm and I had a backlog of chores waiting. That didn't stop me driving straight over with Holly. If April was going to sit below the cairn all day again then I wanted to make sure she was warm and comfortable, with at least water on hand and food, even if she wouldn't eat it.

Mum had called the previous night to ask what was going on at Rainbow, as had my mate Ben and, to my bemusement, Junior. The answer they all received was the same, albeit a bit more abbreviated for Ben and Junior. Mum was less tolerant of my monosyllabic answers and more accomplished at interrogation. I told the truth anyway: I didn't know what the story was with JOY or why April had to watch it, but she seemed fine and I was keeping a close eye on things.

Having known from his dealings with her that April was more than a little eccentric, Junior found it all hilarious and wondered what trick she'd play next. Mum reserved judgement but I could tell from her tone she was worried.

Junior's comment had kept me from falling asleep for some time. The satin wouldn't last that long, not once the weather deteriorated again. The wind would eventually cause the straw to catch the fabric and pierce holes, and the seams to tear. With heavy rain the frames would sink, the bales might sag, and although April's design meant they were wedged in well, the installation had a finite life. Would she pull it down or was part of her strange worship also meant to include its decay as well?

I wondered if I'd have the courage to ask but knew I wouldn't. Wait is what I'd do. Wait and act when necessary.

The following morning I arrived at the cairn in my ute with a rubber-backed blanket and my oilskin, and another thermos, a large bottle of water, sandwiches, and an apple and orange. Perhaps she'd shun the sandwiches again but a bit of fruit might prove harder to resist. And they were colourful, which somehow made them apt.

She'd changed clothes and today wore bright orange trousers tucked into red rubber boots. Her hat and scarf were different too, this time purple, and clashed magnificently with her emerald coat.

I'd hoped she would have laid out a blanket. Instead she'd spread an old nylon chaff bag on the ground. Fine for short-term protection, but the cold would soon seep through along with the damp. Any more days of sitting like that and April would be likely to come down with pneumonia.

'I have something better,' I told her when I'd handed over the food and drink. I returned with the blanket and asked her to stand for a moment while I laid it on top of the chaff bag.

She sat back down and studied my face. 'Why are you doing this, Tristan? You don't have to.'

I scratched my chin and considered how to answer.

She smiled. 'Looking after me isn't in your contract, you know.'

'I can't leave you cold.'

Her gaze shifted back to the paddock. 'I'll never be cold here.'

'Will you stay all day again?'

'Yes.'

I nodded and shoved my hands in my pockets and gazed westward, sniffing as the cold air made my nose drip. 'There's weather coming.' I glanced back at her and wished I hadn't spoken.

Though her focus on JOY remained fixed, April's mouth had dropped and her eyes were filled with unfathomable sadness. 'I don't want it to rain.'

'I know.'

She tilted her head back, her profile lit by the sun, and so tragically beautiful it made my breath catch. 'I'm doing my best.'

The words weren't meant for me.

Overcome, I crouched beside her and touched her face with the back of my fingers. Her eyes flicked open and she held my gaze for so long and so intensely I thought she might reach for my jaw and draw me close enough to kiss. Instead, she smiled wearily and brought her hand to mine, cupping my fingers before gently easing them away.

'I'm so glad you answered my ad.'

'So am I.'

I left and let the balloons attached to my heart carry me weightless for the rest of the day. I checked on April often from Rainbow but only ventured over at lunchtime to make sure she'd eaten. To my relief she'd had half a sandwich and an apple, and also drunk most of her tea. I took the empty thermos and dashed home to refill it, catching another phone call from my mother while I waited for the kettle.

'What is she doing?' Mum demanded.

'I don't know.' But it mattered to April and that's all I cared about.

'Do you think she's ill?' When I didn't answer, Mum let out a frustrated sigh. 'You know this isn't normal.'

'She seems okay to me.'

'Hmm.'

The kettle clicked off and I'd never felt so grateful toward an inanimate object before. 'I have to go, Mum.'

'Keep an eye on her, Tristan. I'm not sure she's well. Your father said she was out by the cairn when he drove to Hamilton this morning and was still there on his return.'

'I'm keeping check.'

But sometimes even the best intentions aren't enough.

And sometimes people don't want to be helped, even by those who love them.

NINE

The storm hit overnight, slapping the land in violent squalls. As soon as it was light I scrambled out of bed and headed out with Holly into an ugly dawn.

I'd been following the weather closely, checking the Bureau's website for warnings. The forecast was for the wildest weather to stay along the coast, but overnight the wind had shifted to straight southerly and pushed the storm front inland. I cursed myself for not paying more attention and following my gut. The sheep weren't in the most exposed paddock but there were safer places on Rainbow, and I wanted them shifted before the weather turned any fouler.

By the time Holly and I had moved the sheep we were soaked and shivering. I let her into the cab and turned the heater up, my fingers like purple sausages on the wheel. We bumped and splashed our way down Rainbow's lanes toward the cottage, sharing glances like we knew what the other was thinking.

My mind was on April and how she'd react to the rain. Although the day held some light, it was so murky and dismal even JOY couldn't brighten it. My stomach lurched at the thought she might be back maintaining vigil below the cairn. She couldn't be. It was too cold, visibility too poor, the squalls and wind gusts too savage. You'd have to be insane to be out in it.

I swallowed and looked at Holly, and turned the ute away from the cottage toward the main house, my gut churning.

The Range Rover was gone.

Holly nearly tipped to the floor as I skidded out of the drive and raced for the road. I barely glanced to check it was clear before accelerating across the bitumen and onto the tourist track. I slid to a halt at the top of the rise and bolted out, leaving the ute's engine running and the door open.

I didn't ask, didn't speak. I didn't care if she fought or bit or screamed, she wasn't staying there. April did none of those things. She shivered and sobbed and buried her face into my wet coat as I carried her to the car and lay her gently inside. I ordered Holly onto her lap and she cuddled the dog hard to her chest as we skidded back to Rainbow.

Unsure if she would have all I needed to warm her or a decent fire going, I ignored the main house and drove to the cottage. Ordering Holly out of the ute, I gathered April up again and carried her inside. She tried to stop me but I was too scared she'd run, and too pumped with adrenaline to let anything other than the Neanderthal in me have his way.

Knowing I'd need warmth and a place to dry off once I'd sorted the sheep, I'd left my fire well stoked. With its thick walls and small interior holding in the heat, the cottage was like walking into a sauna after the ravages of outside. I lowered April to her feet as close to the firescreen as I dared and snatched up the blanket that hung over the back of the couch. Something thicker would have been better, but it was wool and well made by my gran, and the closest to hand. I wrapped it around April's shoulders and ordered her to stay.

The kettle seemed to take ages to boil. I picked up the jug the moment it began to steam and poured its contents into a bucket I'd fetched from the laundry. After a quick finger dip I added more cold until there was no risk of scalding, and carried it back to the fire.

April was sitting on the floor, her gaze on the flames and her expression vacant. I crouched next to her and took her mottled pink and blue hands in mine. 'I'm going to put your hands in the water to warm them up.'

She didn't react. Nor did she pull away when I dipped her fingers into the bucket. After the cold the temperature change must have stung, but except for a slight wrinkle of her brow and twitch of her lips she remained still. I massaged her hands, trying to force warmth into them, scared and angry and so many things.

I wanted to speak but was too afraid that my fear would make me harsh. So I stayed silent, working her hands and watching her face until I'd calmed enough to talk.

'You need to get changed.'

She kept staring at the flames.

'How about a shower? That'll warm you up.'

The fire let out a pop as a pocket of sap exploded.

'You can borrow some of my clothes.'

Again nothing.

'Let me help. Please.'

Slowly, April turned toward me. A tear bubbled and spilled from her left eye. 'Save JOY.'

'I can't. The storm's too strong.' I stroked away the tear. My throat aching from helplessness. 'I can only save you.'

She turned back to the fire and resumed her silent stare. I did the only thing I could do and carried her to the bathroom. After placing her down, I flicked open the shower curtain and turned on the taps then held her firmly by the shoulders.

'I can undress you or you can, but either way you're getting out of those wet clothes and having a hot shower.' I held her gaze. 'Understand?'

April was the first to look away. 'Yes.'

I let her go and waited with my hands on my hips, determined to get my way. She turned her back and removed the emerald parka, then her jumper, shoes, socks and jeans, until she stood like a skinny, shivering child in her underpants and T-shirt.

Satisfied she was going to carry on, I gathered up her things and paused at the doorway. 'There's soap and shampoo you can use. I'll bring you back some clean clothes and a towel in a tick, okay? I'll knock first before I come in to give you time to check the curtain's properly closed.' I hesitated for a second. 'You're safe with me. I promise.'

'I know.'

I nodded and left.

Although it was still early in the day I raided the freezer for a container of the pea and ham soup that Mum had made for me, and programmed the microwave for defrost. I set the kitchen table with placemats and cutlery, and put a pot of proper tea on to brew. Sliced bread stood in the toaster ready to be popped down once the soup was ready.

April took her time emerging but that was fine. The fear that she'd run was gone now. She was warm, dry and, most of all, protected. I could only hope the shower had helped clear her head as well.

Thanks to the thick socks I'd loaned her, I didn't hear April's return until she was nearly at the fire. She'd rolled the hems of my jeans up so much the cuffs swung heavily against her ankles when she walked. The jeans were baggy around her slim hips and cinched in with a plaited roo-skin belt that used rings instead of buckles and could adjust to any size. The excess hung down the jeans front like a long brown tongue. She'd turned the sleeves on the thick polar fleece I'd given her up to her wrists and her skin showed a healthy pale pink glow now the blood was back circulating.

She stood beside me and stared at the fire. I let her be, figuring she'd talk if she wanted, and I'd said more already that morning than I had in all the time I'd known her. There didn't seem much to talk about anyway, other than her trying kill herself with cold.

The microwave beeped and I left her to give it another stir and put the toast on. I made us both mugs of tea and placed them on the table, and carried the teapot over too. When the soup and toast were ready I dished them out and set them down, then crossed to April.

'Come on.'

She let me lead her to the table and sat, blinking at the steaming bowl.

I buttered some toast for her and picked up her spoon and put it into her hand. 'Eat.'

She did as she was told, and we ate our meal, with the wind howling and the rain spattering fat droplets onto the windows, while my mind cast out to the front paddock, thinking of JOY, wondering if it would survive.

But mostly wondering if April would.

TEN

April settled her spoon in her half-finished soup. 'I'd like to go home now, Tristan.'

I shook my head and kept eating, but my gaze slid toward her, alert for any attempt to escape. Not a chance in hell I'd let her back out into that weather.

She reached across for my hand. 'You've done enough.'

Her fingers were soft and warm, and the touch made my heart flip-flop with longing. I didn't want to take her home. I wanted to take her to bed, hold her next to me, all silky and delicate and wild. I wanted to make whatever was hurting her so badly disappear, dissolved by my embrace and strength.

I stared at my soup, torn. I had no right to keep her here. No right to understand her demons. The only rights I had were those dictated in our contract and, while unconventional, I doubted it lacked an escape clause should she want to terminate it. Junior would have seen to that.

She gave my fingers another squeeze. 'I'll be fine.'

I looked at her, and saw an expression full of understanding at my concern. She seemed normal now, as though the morning was an aberration instead of something I'd suspected was inevitable.

'Is there anyone I can call for you? Your mum maybe? Other family?'

'No.' She looked away, something crossing her face that I didn't understand. 'No. I'm better on my own.'

'No one is better on their own.'

She bit her lip and I could have thumped myself for upsetting her.

'April . . .'

She pushed her chair back and stood with her palms wrapped together. 'Please, Tristan.'

I looked down, not liking this at all. But what else could I do? I breathed out, loud enough for her to hear the resignation in it. 'All right.'

She said nothing on the drive home, staring out the passenger window at the flattened landscape. A rain-blurred expanse of endless green and mud.

Another squall hit as I turned into her drive, the drops loud against the ute roof. I parked as close as possible to the shelter of the verandah. As soon as I braked she was out, the door slamming on my call for her to stop. I swore and followed, rain splattering my head and face as I sprinted around the car to catch her before she escaped inside and shut me out again.

'April!'

The door was almost closed when I grabbed it. Her eyes were enormous and bright green against the tangle of her dark hair and pale skin. I could feel her skittery tension as though it were electricity in the air.

She gathered herself, regarding me almost

coldly. 'Thank you for your help, Tristan. You can go now.'

It must have been the tone that got me. I'm not one for answering back but I wasn't about to be dismissed like that. 'I'm not your bloody servant.'

She dropped her head.

'I'm your friend, April.' I glanced over her head at the sliver of interior I could see. The house was dark and unfriendly. I didn't want to leave her there alone. 'Is your fire lit?'

'I don't know.'

'Can I check?'

She let out a breath and, without looking at me, stood aside and held the door open. It wasn't an invitation as such but I took it as one. I kicked off my boots and walked into a hallway that felt devoid of any sense of home. No colour, no warmth, no scent of life, no lingering echoes of laughter. All stale shadows and loneliness.

She walked with the cuffs of my jeans flopping about her ankles, and turned into a doorway on the right. I followed her into a large, surprisingly modern kitchen-dining area, divided by a breakfast bar. April moved past it to a cold fireplace. Timber was stacked in a neat pile next to the hearth, along with a pile of old newspapers and a box of firelighters. Without a fire crackling, the room seemed as lifeless as the hall.

April was at the sink, staring out of the kitchen window to the east, and I was glad that the kitchen didn't face south, where she would be accosted with JOY as it sank into the ground. That didn't mean other rooms wouldn't have a view. I felt a surge of anxiety at what it would do to April when she was challenged once more with the destruction of her art.

If art was what it was. I had the feeling that whatever the purpose of April's installation, it wasn't for art's sake, but for her own. Or, perhaps, for someone else's. Someone that existed only in her head.

Or perhaps the sky she continually regarded with sad, hollow eyes.

I crouched at the fire and began to set kindling and logs, while thinking of things to say to her. Or ask. But the impetus was gone and I was back to my tongue-tied self, and I was beginning to feel uncomfortable about the way I'd forced myself inside. The more I contemplated it the more I was troubled that my presence might make her nervous. That she might begin to think I wasn't to be trusted. She was alone, isolated. I was bigger, stronger and obviously had feelings for her. What woman wouldn't get nervous?

I lit the fire and waited to make sure it caught, then stood and brushed my hands down jeans that were still damp from the morning. I hadn't had a chance to change, and with everything else bothering me I began to feel the cold like dread.

'Do you have food? Milk?'

April nodded. 'I bought groceries the other day.'

'Okay.' I stood awkwardly, wanting to escape, but wanting reassurance that she'd be all right on her own. 'If you need anything call me.'

'I'll manage.'

I realised then that her car was still across the road. 'Do you have your car keys?'

She frowned and shook her head. 'No. They're with my clothes.' Which were still at the cottage, in the laundry.

'Okay. As soon as there's a break I'll bring your car back.'

'Thanks.' She smiled a little and rubbed her hair away from her face.

'You're tired.'

'A bit.'

'You should sleep.'

'I should do a lot of things.' Suddenly she sobbed and turned to the window.

I was behind her in a few strides, touching her shoulders and turning her to my chest. 'Don't cry, April. Please don't cry.'

She rested her head and let me stroke her hair as I shushed and talked softly, promising her everything would be fine when I had no idea what was wrong in the first place.

'I hurt so much.'

'I know.'

'I'm trying to make it better, I really am.'

'You will. You're strong and brave and beautiful. You'll make it right.'

We stood in the dull kitchen light with the fire crackling behind us for what was the saddest and most beautiful moment of my life. Finally, she sniffed and pulled away, not meeting my eyes. 'I think I'll go sleep now.'

'Do you want me to stay?'

'No, but thanks for the offer. I just need rest.'

I let her walk away, her movements like a fragile old lady whose bones needed care. The floorboards moaned her passage. A door further along the hall closed. I let out a long sigh and studied the kitchen. Now that I was paying attention, I could see there was food. Baskets of potatoes and onions. A glass jar of biscuits. Some oranges in a bowl. I checked the fridge anyway. A packet of ham. Another of cheese. Milk. She wouldn't starve.

I tossed another chunk of wood on the fire and placed the guard around it. Along the mantel above was a line of little metal cars. Not commercial Matchbox types but handcrafted ones of fabulous design. April's work I guessed. They were whimsical and fun, the sort of art that someone who danced in paddocks would produce.

An ache flooded me. Even if I never got to hold her again, if I never kissed her or made love with her, or shared anything of what pulsed in my heart, I wanted that dancing, laughing girl back.

Without her, the world seemed too dark.

ELEVEN

I didn't see April for three days. The weather passed, blown away as it always is by winter winds, but the land remained chilled and soggy. Mum and Andrea came to visit, taking it upon themselves to knock beforehand on April's door with a plan to introduce themselves. A plan they failed to advise me of and which left me mute with anger when they told me on arrival at the cottage.

I hadn't revealed to anyone what happened that morning. I didn't want anyone thinking unfair things about April. Already I could feel the whispers around town, about her eccentricity, about JOY and what it could mean. Innuendoes that April was somehow not quite with it. I never commented, but for me that was normal behaviour and a surprise to no one. Though without anyone to dispute their assertions the gossipmongers continued on their petty way, telling their tales. I hurt on April's behalf but remained silent.

Better to do that than reveal the truth.

JOY was now gone. The day after April's heartbreak, sick of waiting for the weather to ease, I rugged up as best I could, braved the rain and wind and pulled the installation down. The frames

I shifted to the back of the main shed, away from sight of the house. The bales I stripped of their fabric and left in a stack with the frames. Later, when I felt the time was right, I'd ask April if I could use some of the straw for mulch around the cottage.

A muddy strip was now the only sign that JOY had ever existed. Each time I neared the paddock the sight of it left a heavy feeling in my gut. Instinct told me I'd done the right thing, but my heart clenched with worry that I'd destroyed April's precious work, her message to I don't know what – God, the world. Who knew? The longer she remained hidden from me, suffering in the house alone, the worse my fear became.

Andrea was cranky that April refused to answer the door, calling her stuck up. Mum, being Mum, leaned toward worry and made me promise to check on April later and report back.

'What happened to the letters?' asked Mum as she sat in the cottage, slicing the fruitcake she'd brought while tea brewed in the pot.

'Storm broke it.'

'What were they for?' asked Andrea.

I shrugged.

'Do you know anything about her?' When I didn't answer Andrea rolled her eyes. 'You're completely hopeless.'

'I just work here.'

Mum gave me one of her looks. I busied myself with mugs. She knew I was hiding something but she also knew I wouldn't say a word in front of Andrea. I wondered how long she'd give me before returning on her own to quiz me properly. Not long I suspected.

As soon as they'd gone I drove up to the main shed and hung around, servicing the quad bike, hoping for a glimpse of April. I knew she was home. The Range Rover was in the shed and smoke trailed from the chimney. A pair of bright yellow rubber boots had appeared beside the door, mud caked to their heels. She'd been out and I'd missed her.

I was just about to give up and go banging on her door when she appeared. She wore jeans and the yellow boots and a fleece-lined leather bomber jacket. With her hair tied back in a loose pony tail she appeared sexy and young, like a girl from 50s America. She was carrying a parcel of folded clothes and I realised I'd forgotten about the jeans and jumper I'd loaned her.

My heart skipped at the sight of her.

'Hello, Tristan.' She proffered the clothes. 'I thought I'd better return these.'

I held up my greasy hands.

April laughed. 'I'll put them in your ute then.'

Her jeans were tight and hugged her bum, creases forming around the globes as she walked. No longer the lost little girl standing shivering in my bathroom. An adult. Confident. Laughing. I wanted her so badly it hurt.

She returned to me and studied the quad bike with her lips pursed. 'Is there something wrong with it?'

I shook my head, cheeks hot thanks to where my thoughts had drifted. I couldn't stop looking at her, how healthy she looked. How normal.

'Was that your mum who knocked on my door?'

'And sister.'

'I was in the shower. By the time I was decent they were gone.' She smiled. 'They probably think I was avoiding them on purpose.'

'No.'

She looked around and I began to fret she was looking for JOY, but when she returned her gaze to mine her expression was friendly. Even, I imagined, a little bit tender.

'Can you do something for me?' she said.

'Sure.'

'I want to buy some sheep.'

I turned that over in my mind. Sheep. Harmless, surely. 'What sort?'

'I'd like those ones with black faces and legs.' She cocked onto one hip and tilted her head, thinking. 'Short wool, I think, too. Or newly shorn.'

'Not the right time for newly shorn.'

'No, I suppose not.'

I considered for a while. 'I might be able to find you some Suffolks. Ewes?'

'I guess. Would you be able to use ewes when I've finished?'

'Depends on what you've done to them.'

She laughed and touched my arm. 'Nothing too traumatic. In fact, I think the sheep will quite enjoy it.'

Though her touch was warming, worry twisted my gut. She read it in my face.

'Don't, Tristan.' Her voice was soft and pleading. 'I have to do this.'

'Why?'

She turned away to look at the hills, biting her lip. 'Because I just do.' She shook her head. 'You wouldn't understand.'

'I might, if you explained.'

Her hand went to the top of her chest, fingers splaying. 'I can't. Not yet.'

'Okay.' I let it drop, comforted a little by the 'not yet', which was far better than a 'not ever'. 'Let me know how many you need and I'll see what I can arrange.'

'Thanks.' She turned to leave and then whirled back. 'Oh, I meant to ask, does the farm have one of those old-fashioned sheep dips? The sort where you run the sheep through a big trough?'

'No. It used to, but it looks like it was filled in when they replaced the old yards.'

'Oh. Bugger.' She scratched at her neck. 'Could you build a temporary one? Using portable yards and maybe a sunken old bath or something?'

I took a while answering. I could build anything if I put my mind to it, but whether I should in this case was another matter. 'What do you want it for?'

'You'll see. Can you do it?'

'Maybe. I'll have a think about it.' Feeling brave, I held her gaze. 'Why don't you come over for dinner tonight and we can work something out? You can pick up your clothes at the same time.'

My heart sank as her head lowered.

She was quiet a long time. 'That's sweet of you, but no. I don't think it's a good idea.'

Baboon's bum exploded in full force. I bent to gather the tools I'd had out and stacked them into my tool box. What an idiot. I may as well have come out and asked her for a shag. She'd have to be blind to not see how I felt. It'd been innocent though. Dinner, that was all. Just a normal meal in the cottage and some normal chat.

Idiot. Idiot. Idiot.

'Tristan.'

I snapped the toolbox closed and carried it to the ute, not daring to look at her. I dumped it in the back, whistling for Holly. One of the northern paddock gates wasn't hanging right and I wanted to fix it. Then I'd go into town and do something. Buy groceries. Maybe call in to see Ben, have a couple of beers. Stay away from Rainbow.

She walked to the ute. 'It's not because I don't want to.'

I stared at the ground, wanting to melt away. I wasn't stupid. I knew when I was being humoured.

'Tristan, will you look at me? Please?'

She was close. Too close. Right in my personal space, smelling of sweet things, of my hopes. I was so lost.

She cupped a hand around my jaw. 'Hey.'

I stared at her and drowned in those sad green eyes.

'Not yet, okay?' And I knew she was talking about us and not her secret hurt. That she had something to get through and if I was there, if I stood close and helped her, then maybe we could be something.

I just had to wait.

TWELVE

I found April her sheep, all one hundred and fifty head. At a price. I still had no real idea what April planned with the Suffolks but I didn't think it would be as weather contingent as JOY. Sheep were, after all, pretty hardy and not prone to collapsing at the first sign of rain.

She was back welding again. A delivery of sheet metal had arrived and each day saw April at work in the shed. At first I had no clue what she was up to, but by the time the sheep arrived and her creations began to take form I had a fair idea.

The sheep were let loose in a good sheltered paddock not far from the main house. Often I'd pass to find April leaning on the gate, watching them with her welder's face mask tipped back and a smile on her face. Sometimes I stopped to talk, other times I waved and moved on, busy with my own chores. It gave me daydreams though. April as a farmer's wife. Happy at Rainbow, with me.

Mum caught me on one of the days when I'd stopped to chat with April, spying us as she drove toward the cottage and quickly changing direction.

'You must be April,' she said, striding down to meet us with her hand thrust out. 'I'm Tristan's mum, Christine. So glad to meet you at last.'

I held my breath as April returned the greeting, feeling teenaged and squirmy embarrassed, as if Mum had caught me kissing someone I shouldn't have been behind the shearing shed.

'Hello, Mrs Blake.'

Mum shooed her away. 'Oh, enough of that. Call me Christine.' She lasered her shrewd gaze on me. 'You never mentioned April was so pretty. Or so young.'

I couldn't look at her let alone answer.

April laughed. 'I can't imagine Tristan saying much about anything.'

'No. Our boy's not much of a talker.'

I waved toward the cottage, desperately trying to control my rising blush and failing badly. Mum knew I hated being talked about like this. In front of April only made it worse. 'Cuppa?'

Mum looked at April. 'You'll join us?'

April shook her head. 'No. I still have some chores to complete. It was nice to meet you though. Tristan has mentioned you a couple of times. I think he's very proud of the women in his family.'

It was Mum's turn to laugh. 'Yes, we do tend to be a bit formidable. Probably why Tristan's so shy around women. He knows what we're capable of.'

'Mum.'

She merely smiled and exchanged a conspiratorial wink with April.

I whistled for Holly who was off sniffing mice holes in the grass. 'I'll put the kettle on.'

'You do that. I'll be over in a minute.'

I shared a look with April but she seemed

unfazed. Still I hesitated. Mum could be overbearing when the mood took her, and she didn't understand how fragile April was, how much I needed to look after her.

Mum cocked her eyebrows. 'Well?'

I opened my mouth, closed it, looked at Holly, then looked back at April whose eyes seemed full of sympathy. I forced myself to walk and not glance back.

Mum turned up ten minutes later and plonked herself at the dining table, studying me in that way she had, seeing too much.

'You like her.'

I said nothing. Better than letting Mum hear how I really felt. I placed a plate of fruitcake on the table and returned for our mugs.

'Did you know she was an artist?' Mum said as I set her mug in front of her and sat down.

'I guessed.'

'She's planning another display.' She picked off the corner of some fruitcake and popped it in her mouth, all the time her eyes on me. 'You're helping her, I take it?'

'Only when she asks. It's part of the contract.'

'How you feel about her isn't though.' There was no tease in her voice. She didn't like it. 'Tristan, you need to be careful.'

I took a sip of tea. Mum had no idea. April was too precious to be anything but careful with.

She curled her hand around my arm. 'She won't stay here. Not forever. And then where will you be?'

The same thought had occurred to me a

hundred times. I knew it was a possibility. That once she'd purged herself, made whatever it was better, she'd leave. Except April had given me a 'not yet' promise and I wasn't going to let it go. 'She might.'

'Oh, Tristan. You're too hopeful for your own good sometimes.' She sighed. 'Fortunately she seems a nice girl. Pretty in her own way.'

Not pretty. Beautiful. And in every way.

'You should ask her over home for dinner one night.'

'She's my boss, Mum.' Plus I knew April would say no. Dinners and everything else would have to wait until 'not yet' had become 'now'. And I didn't know when that would be.

'All the more reason to have her over.' She tilted her head. 'Do you want me to ask?'

'She won't go.'

'Why not?'

'She just won't.'

'Of course she will.'

'Look, just leave it, will you?' I stared at the cake. I never yelled at Mum. I never yelled at anyone unless it was on the footy field. 'Sorry.'

'What are you hiding, Tristan?'

I stood and dumped the contents of my half drunk mug into the sink. 'I have work to do.'

The way I'd spoken to Mum, the fear I had for April, stayed with me all week. I avoided April, and only spoke the necessities when I went into town. My conscience wrestled with itself. I knew April wasn't well but I thought Rainbow, her art and I could help her.

On Friday, April hopped into her Range Rover and tracked me down at the far reaches of the farm, where a small creek ran between the gully of two hills, and where some of the land was showing slippage. I wasn't doing anything except staring and thinking. The erosion around the creek was the worst, and I wanted to put a rehabilitation strategy in place before the property was fully restocked. But that would take money, and I didn't own the land, nor did I know how April felt about this aspect of farm management. Perhaps she didn't even care.

I hated that thought. I wanted her to care. I wanted her to feel about Rainbow the same way I did.

The weather had turned unseasonably mild, like a tease. It was still cold, but if I stood leeward of the wind, in a patch of sun, I could almost taste spring.

The rumble of her engine had me glancing up. Sunlight glittered across the Range Rover's metallic duco, turning the red to flames. April pulled up next to my ute and stepped out, wearing the jeans and bomber jacket that made my stomach clench and forced me to cross my arms and jam them there so I didn't try to touch her.

'You look busy.'

I nodded toward the hill. 'Bad erosion.'

She rested her bum next to mine on the ute's bull bar and studied the hill. 'And you want to do something about it.'

'Yes.' She waited for me to continue and I tried to formulate a way to describe what I wanted from her without coming across as mercenary or pleading. Nothing sounded right. I sighed, disheartened with myself and blabbed the truth. 'I can't afford to fix it.'

'Do what needs to be done. I'll sort the rest.'

'I'm meant to be running Rainbow.'

'You are, but that's a capital expense. My responsibility.'

'I wasn't sure you'd care.'

'It took me nine months to find this property, Tristan. To find a place that called to me, that had all the things I needed. Believe me, I care.'

I couldn't help my smile as I regarded the slope and began mentally listing priorities.

'You've been avoiding me since your Mum's visit.'

My smile dropped.

'She was fine. She wanted to make sure I'd settled in okay, mentioned a few shops I might try in Hamilton if I needed anything special. She even invited me to join the Rannoch branch of the Country Women's Association.'

That didn't surprise me. Mum invited everyone to join the CWA. Blake women had a proud history of membership.

'She cares about you very much.'

'Mum cares about all of us. It's what she does.' I glanced at her. 'Did you say yes?'

'To the CWA?' She grinned. 'No. I'm not much of a cook.'

'They do a lot more than cook.'

'I know.' Her head dropped. 'I'm good for some things but not that. Not yet.'

I couldn't help it. The sadness in her voice made me do it. I wrapped an arm around her and pulled her close. 'You will be. One day.'

She looked up at me in a way that made me want to kiss her, and for a moment we both hesitated. There was an electric hum in the air as the tension spiked. My gaze dropped to her mouth and her lips parted. My breath came faster and Mum's warning, April's plea for patience, were forgotten as the need to kiss her swamped me.

I began to lower my head, but April pulled away. She straightened and hugged herself, and gazed at me with eyes pleading for understanding.

'I can't, Tristan. I still hurt too much.'

'Did someone do this to you?'

'Yes.' At my look of fury she held up a hand and hurried on. 'But it's not what you think.'

My hands were in fists, my jaw clenched. Whoever had hurt her had better stay a long way away from me. And even further from April.

'Please, forget it.'

'I don't want to. I hate the thought of anyone hurting you.'

'It's the price we pay for love, Tristan. Sometimes it crushes us.'

'I would never hurt you. Never.'

'I know.' She smiled sadly and then flapped her arms out from her sides and let them drop back. 'I didn't mean for this to happen. This . . .' She gave up but I knew what she meant. This conversation, this escalation of feeling. These revelations. 'I came to find you because I wanted help with the sheep.'

I tried to hide my disappointment. 'We'll need Holly then.' I whistled for the dog.

Her relief that the moment was over only made it worse. But there was one thing I possessed plenty of, and that was patience.

Although even my reserves were nearly drained when April explained what she wanted to do to her expensive flock of stud Suffolk ewes.

THIRTEEN

April wanted to dye her sheep. In rainbow colours, using wool-fast vegetable dye.

I paced the shed while she stood watching me with her arms crossed. 'No.'

'No?'

I halted. 'You can't. It'll wreck the wool.'

'It won't. The dye is made of perfectly natural materials. It won't hurt the sheep or the wool. They'll simply be coloured.'

I wanted to explain to her that everyone would think she was crazy, that they'd whisper even more about her. That they wouldn't understand. 'And then what?'

'And then I'll move them to the front paddock. They'll be happy.' She giggled and pressed her hands together in front of her face, bouncing a little with the excitement of it. 'Literally.'

I scraped my hand over my head. I knew what the sheet metal was for now. I understood her, I saw the thrill her creation gave her. I heard her giggle and saw the brightness in her eyes. The pure hope there.

I dropped my hand and sighed heavily. So what if everyone thought she was nuts? I knew the truth and so did April, I think. 'Okay.'

She squealed and ran up to me, wrapped her hands around my face and reached up on tip-toes to kiss me lightly on the mouth. 'Thank you.'

A kiss. A light brush of her lips against mine. Tiny, friendly, but with that one touch I would have given her anything.

She let me go and began to twirl, her loose hair spilling out like a silken shroud, catching the sun. Everything inside me lurched, like that feeling you get when an elevator drops too fast. If I wasn't lost before I was then.

Crazy love like I'd never felt before.

Dyeing the sheep wasn't easy. In fact I think it was the most frustrating thing I'd ever done with any form of livestock, and that includes the time I had to help a mate with his experimental deer herd. April's Suffolk ewes weren't as bad as that, but if you've ever attempted to dye an animal that doesn't want to be coloured bright blue or red or yellow, you'd understand.

After April's initial inquiry about the old sheep dip, I'd given the idea a bit of thought. We could have sunk a large drum, split sideways, or bought a plastic trough for the job and that would have been fine had April wanted all the sheep the same colour. But the plan was for an ovine rainbow which meant small batches of dye and small lots of sheep. We had a hundred and fifty head and seven colours. And they all needed to be done in quick succession so that each animal remained as vibrantly coloured as the next.

We ended up with the sheep separated out into mobs in portable yards. I built a series of races and bought seven deep plastic dog washing tubs from a pet supplies, which April filled with dye. Each sheep was manhandled into the tub and soaked for a good few minutes, before being hoisted out and let go, usually bleating in indignation.

By the time we were finished, Holly, April and I looked like escapees from a hippy commune. Holly had turned a strange combination of colours, blue in some spots, a few touches of green, and a patch of alarming purple on one ear, but the rest of her coat was a muddy brown.

April's hair, being dark, remained unscathed, but one eyebrow had turned a sickly greeny yellow and her hands were mottled from the tips of her fingers to her elbows. Mine were the same, along with my clothes and my hat, and from the way April kept developing the giggles each time she looked at me I knew there was something going on with my face. I didn't mind, and to see her having fun made up for the sheer frustration of the day.

The sheep looked amazing though. Black tipped but with bodies unnaturally vibrant. And somehow, despite my fatigue, despite the stupidness of it, looking at them made me happy. They made me want to laugh and brought a little bit of frivolous joy to the world. If making people smile was April's goal then I had no doubt she'd fulfil it.

'They don't seem to mind,' she said, leaning her bum against a rail and observing them.

'They probably don't see each other the same as we see them.'

'Are they colour-blind?'

'No, but their colour perception isn't as good as ours.'

She slid me a sideways look. 'You know a lot about sheep.'

'A bit. Not as much as Dad or Gramps though.' I matched her sneaky look. 'Anyway I thought that's why you hired me?'

'I did. But you had other qualities that I liked as well.'

'How did you know? You'd never even met me.'

'I had references.' She gave me another look. 'And I did some nosing.'

Holly placed her head between my knees and I bent down to stroke her. 'So you know everything about me and I know nothing about you?'

'You know all you need to about me. The rest doesn't matter.'

'Everything about you matters.'

She didn't reply to that but I could see a faint smile quirking her mouth and knew I'd said something good. It made me wonder what she'd say if I revealed to her the emotion sitting fat and throbbing in my heart.

I glanced at the sky. 'So now what?'

'We put them somewhere they can't get too dirty. Then you can come and help me with the troughs.'

That was what the sheet metal had been turned into – feed troughs for the sheep. We loaded them onto the tractor and carted them to the paddock. I was surprised she hadn't asked me to mow the area first. Since JOY the grass had re-established itself. The cleared patch was still a slightly different colour and the pasture wasn't back to its full height, but it was thick enough.

When I asked she shook her head. 'I need the contrast.'

Using builder's string and wooden posts, April measured out the top and bottom of the installation. Then she closed off one end with more string to create an open ended rectangle. I expected her to divide the rectangle into more boxes but when I asked she simply smiled and said, 'You'll see.'

Following April's instructions, I dragged the troughs into line, while she measured and tweaked, until a 'H' and then an 'A' were spelled perfectly across the grass. Not an angle or parallel was out of line, the joins seamless. I marvelled at the cleverness of it.

'Basic trigonometry,' she said, clapping her hands together. 'The nuns would be impressed.' She turned to me. 'I went to a very expensive school.'

'You're Catholic?'

'I'm nothing.' Her expression turned harsh. 'God doesn't exist. If he did he . . .' She squeezed her eyes shut. Her entire body stiffening as though she was fighting some sort of rage or grief.

'April?'

She opened her eyes and forced a patently fake smile. 'Sorry. I have a thing about religion these days.' She pressed her hand over her mouth. 'You're not religious, are you?'

'Not really. It's not something I think about much.' I surveyed the landscape. 'I believe in nature though. It's not always kind but it's true.'

'I believe in nature too.' She frowned a little. 'I think … I think our spirits live in it somehow, when we're gone. That we're not really gone but out there, somewhere. Not whole, but … there.' She paused and then looked at me and shook her head. 'How did we get onto this?'

'Trigonometry.'

'Of course. Trigonometry. No wonder I hated it at school.' She hauled another trough in place, closing the subject. Together we worked until they were all laid out and aligned as she wanted.

When the 'Y' was in place, April walked to the bottom of the paddock. I followed, joining her to look back at the word we'd made.

HAPPY stretched across the paddock, the fresh metal silvery in the sun.

And in that moment I forgot my feelings about God and religion, and said a heartfelt silent prayer that this word would live up to itself.

FOURTEEN

We let the sheep in the next day.

April had asked me to source appropriate feed and we laid a trail of sheep pellets through the troughs. Not too thick, but enough to keep the sheep occupied for a while. I'd advised April that it would take a bit of trial and error to work out how much we'd need to dole out to keep the sheep there for as long as she needed.

If April had her way, she would have had the sheep feeding all day, but that wouldn't have been good for them. To lessen her disappointment I suggested that shorter bursts of sheep activity would help the installation retain its impact. After all, rainbows didn't linger forever. Part of their magic was that they appeared briefly in our lives, like a blessing, before disappearing into the wind.

My words made her look at me in a way that turned everything inside me liquid and had baboon's bum creeping its way once more up my cheeks.

At eleven, I used Holly and the quad bike to shift the multi-coloured mob into the front paddock. At first they lingered in one corner but Holly soon had them shuffling in the right direction, and once the sheep smelled the pellets they were into it.

April kept clapping her hands and bouncing as they milled and bullied their way to the feed. The moment the sheep were settled around the troughs she sprinted off for her car and drove across to the cairn.

Holly and I exchanged a look and I shrugged, then headed to the cottage for a thermos and the rubber-backed rug.

April was crying when I arrived and I took a moment before deciding they weren't sad tears. I laid out the rug and told her to sit. Her jeans were already soaked and I was sure she was cold, but she was too lost to notice.

Across in the paddock the sheep kept feeding, bunting each other and occasionally milling around and changing positions. Red, yellow, green, blue, orange, purple and pink. Not quite the rainbow spectrum but close.

April was right. They were happy. Literally.

She pulled her knees up to her chest and wrapped her arms around her shins, rocking as though to some silent tune. On the outside she seemed delighted but I couldn't help feeling troubled by her gaze. She kept shifting it to the sky in a way that seemed searching, as if she expected some sign to appear, or perhaps a vision. But it was just the sky. The strange deep cold blue of winter, dotted with lumbering clouds, and speckled with the occasional bird.

Several cars slowed, some almost to a stop as heads popped out of windows to gawk at the sheep. A couple veered onto the cairn road and drove to the top. I hoped they wouldn't disturb us, and I was in luck. Whoever they were, they were too busy laughing and taking photos to care about the people on the slope below.

The sheep stayed in place for close to an hour before they started to get restless and move away. The greedier ones kept searching for pellets, bossing others out of the way to hoover up any remaining scraps. But it wasn't much longer before even they dispersed, leaving the paddock splattered with coloured sheep dots, as if someone had flicked multiple paint brushes at it.

'Is it what you hoped for?' I asked April.

'Yes.' She smiled and wiped her cold-pinked cheeks. 'It was perfect.'

I reached for her hand and squeezed it. 'I'm glad.' Then I stood and whistled for Holly and left April to her thoughts. The display was over, and it was my and Holly's job to move the flock away from the road.

As I drove back I thought of what she'd said: perfect. Perfect was good. Perhaps even enough to ease her hurt and make her world better.

We kept the ritual of HAPPY up for nearly a week, until the sheep turned the ground to mud around the troughs and the vibrant colour of their coats began to fade with rain, wear and dirt. Sensing April was conducting some sort of communion she would rather experience in private, I stopped joining her at the cairn. Several locals, having cottoned on to the ritual, stopped by and tried to get her to talk. I heard no mention that she was anything but polite, but I did hear grumbles around town at her refusal to reveal the purpose of it all.

The local paper came and took photos. When April refused an interview they rang me, which caused nothing but hilarity in my family when I related the story over dinner at Oakvale a few nights later. I didn't find it so funny. Not being a local, the young girl they'd assigned didn't know I wasn't a talker. And she'd seemed genuinely sincere about the community interest in April's project.

'What's it all in aid of anyway?' Dad asked me when everyone had settled back to their meals.

I shrugged. 'Art.'

'With sheep?' said Jeremy.

'Why not?' countered Andrea. 'There's that bloke in England who pickled a cow.'

'Damien Hirst,' I said.

Everyone looked at me.

A blush began to itch at my neck and crept upward. 'April told me about him.'

Jeremy grinned. 'You and April been having a lot of conversations then?'

I mumbled a 'not really' and concentrated on my roast dinner.

Andrea nudged me. 'Liar.'

I didn't bite but I felt Mum's gaze like a laser beam.

'So what's she going to do next?' asked Patrick.

'I don't know.' I looked at him. 'She doesn't tell me. I just help when the time comes.'

Jeremy winked. 'I bet you do, little bro.'

'Are you and her . . . ?' Andrea said, eyebrows wiggling. She was never one to let things go.

It was a question hard to answer. I didn't know what April and I were. I only had moments with her that I hoped meant something. And dreams. So many dreams.

I stared at my plate. 'No.'

'Pull the other one, you big boob,' said Laurie. 'Look at your face.'

'Leave it.'

Everyone shut up. Mum had spoken.

I threw a questioning glance her way, surprised she'd defended me. She gave a subtle shake of her head and although I'd lost all my appetite I returned to my dinner, determined not to make my show of feelings worse.

For a while all we heard was the scrape of cutlery and a distant bark as one of the farm dogs sniffed a rabbit or fox. Then Dad asked Andrea about the Show Society and April was forgotten, but not for long. After shooing the others away, Mum ordered me into the kitchen to help with the dishes.

I stood nervously with a tea towel in my hand, waiting for the interrogation.

'Is everything all right at Rainbow?'

'April said she'll fund the creek rehabilitation that I was telling Dad about.'

'That's good of her.'

It was. Very good of her. I wasn't convinced about the capital expenditure thing, and wondered how much of April's generosity was because she felt obliged, that this was some sort of compensation for not returning my feelings, or whether she truly believed it was her responsibility.

'Are you spending much time with her?'

'No. Only when she needs me.'

'Which is how often?'

'Not very.'

'So you're not . . .?'

I shook my head. My disappointment must have shown because Mum gave me one of her special Mum looks – a mixture of sympathy and understanding, and the promise that everything would work out for the best in the end.

She propped the roasting dish on the drainer and began to wipe down the sink. I left it to drip, my mind on April, wondering what she was doing in the house, how she coped with the lonely nights. If she read or watched telly or knitted or did some other craft. If she liked music and movies.

'I could find her a puppy,' I said suddenly and then stared at the floor in embarrassment when I realised I'd spoken out loud.

Mum didn't seem to notice. 'I'll keep an ear out.' She squeezed the dishcloth out and pulled the plug. She gave me a pointed look. 'It's not healthy for her to be on her own at night like that.'

'She's not ready,' I mumbled. 'Yet.'

Mum's eyebrows shot up. 'Yet? So you've talked. About,' she twirled a hand, looking for the appropriate phrase, 'about getting together?'

I felt like dying. 'Sort of.'

'What do you mean 'sort of'?'

I shook my head and quickly grabbed the roasting pan, wiping as fast as I could. As far as I was concerned the conversation was over. I'd revealed far too much as it was.

She let out a heavy sigh. 'What am I going to do with you?'

'Nothing, Mum. I'm fine as is.'

'You're not. You're completely lovesick over a girl who I fear is only going to break your heart.'

I shrugged. It was my heart. If April broke it then that would be my burden to deal with.

'I'm worried, Tristan. This business is all very strange.'

'Don't be. April's happy.' I dumped the pan onto the benchtop and kissed her cheek. 'And so am I.'

FIFTEEN

April wasn't happy.

It took until PLAY for me to understand that. When I did, the realisation of what she must be going through caused a physical pain inside me. But that was nothing compared to April's suffering. It must have been unbearable for her. I think in the end it became that way.

After HAPPY April retreated into herself again. I sometimes saw her out walking and would stop and ask how she was, let her fuss over Holly while I kept my hands in my pockets so I wouldn't touch her. Once, I caught her chopping firewood and stopped to finish the job for her.

Woodchopping is sweaty work but I like the rhythm of the axe swing and the pull on my body. At Oakvale, my brothers used to think it a lark to pass down the chore to me while they got on with better things, but I never minded. It helped build muscle – muscles that came in handy when laying footy tackles and wrestling with Patrick.

I expected April to leave me to it but she settled on a log to watch while she stroked Holly's head.

'Why are you still single?' she asked.

I shrugged and lined up another block of wood.

'You should be fighting them off with a stick.'

I gave her a wry look. That'd never happened in my life.

'Have you ever had a girlfriend?'

'Of course,' I said, a bit sulky. What did she think I was?

'How many?'

Hoisting the axe, I gave her one of those 'I don't want to talk about it' warning expressions. She backed off, but only a little.

'So where are they now?'

The log split. 'City.'

'Ah. I guess that must happen a lot.'

'A bit.' I placed one of the split halves on the stump and lined it up.

She turned her head away and stared toward the horizon. 'You should try to find a nice local girl.'

I dropped the axe head to the ground and leaned on the shaft, staring at her. When April refused to look at me I let the axe go and crouched in front of her and took her hands. She regarded me with eyes filling with tears.

'Love hurts, Tristan. Really hurts.'

'Not mine.'

She bit her lip and shook her head. 'You're too much.'

'I'm not enough.'

She laughed at that. 'Oh, you're enough, Tristan, believe me.'

I frowned, not understanding.

She cupped a hand around my jaw. 'Do you ever look in the mirror?'

I did, most days when I shaved, but I guess

that's not what she meant.

Wonder spread across her face. 'You really have no idea. Tristan,' she said, this time cupping both palms around my cheeks, 'you're a babe.'

My face turned into a furnace.

She laughed. 'God, you're gorgeous.'

'Then kiss me.'

Her thumb stroked my lips. She studied my eyes, her gaze dropping to my mouth. I couldn't breathe for the anticipation throttling my insides.

April let out a long sigh and my heart sank. It wasn't going to happen. I dropped my head.

She kissed my hair, whispering. 'It's for your own good.'

'You're leaving.'

'No.'

But I heard the 'not yet' in her voice. I was beginning to hate 'not yet'.

'Shit.' I dragged myself from her and went back to the axe. I didn't look at her, I couldn't. She'd seen inside me and rejected it.

The logs spat chunks as I swung. Fast, then faster. Sweat made my hair wet, my shirt soaked. I was so focused I didn't see April leave. Only when the last log was done did I look up and see Holly sitting on her own, her head tilted quizzically at me. I sank onto the stump and buried my face into my hands, feeling a stupid childish urge to cry.

The screen door squeaked open and I turned to see April coming toward me with a large glass of water.

She stood at my side and handed it to me. 'Your job is safe, Tristan.'

I gulped the water and held the empty glass between my hands, rolling the cool surface against my palms. 'What's the point of it if you're not here?'

'I said I wasn't leaving.'

Maybe it was premonition or Mum's warning, I don't know, but I couldn't bring myself to believe her.

'Tristan.'

I sighed and looked up.

'Will you help me?'

My gaze flicked across hers, hopeful.

'I'm going to build PLAY.'

Dismay rolled through me, and though I tried to hide it April noticed.

She touched my cheek. 'I'm sorry but this one's important. It's . . .' A crack formed in her voice. 'It's special. It's for . . . it just means a lot.'

I stood and handed her back the glass. 'I'll help.'

'Thanks.' She squeezed my shoulder and smiled. 'You'll like this one. It's fun.'

'Does it involve animals?'

'Not a single one.' She made a face. 'Well, not real ones.'

That cryptic comment was solved the following afternoon when I turned up at the shed, as arranged, to find April with a gas bottle of helium and a box full of balloons. But not any balloons, these were the foil sort that you put on sticks and came in all kinds of weird shapes.

She was right about the animals, but most were fairy-tale rather than realistic. Purple unicorns, giraffes the colour of daisies, pink dolphins, electric blue elephants. There were also blow-up motorbikes and tractors, and characters from cartoons and computer-generated animated films.

Another box lay open. Inside were windmills – the plastic, glittery sort kids could win at sideshows.

April punched a unicorn my way. It floated past and then shot up to the roof. She laughed and picked up a giant wobbling flower, this time handing it to me.

'Are you throwing a party?'

Something flashed across her face and was gone. 'Not quite, but it should be fun all the same.'

I looked around me. 'So what do you want me for?'

She pointed to the unicorn, bobbing around the roof. 'I need someone to keep all of these under control.'

I considered for a moment. 'Too much chance of escapees out here. Better inside.'

April glanced at the house and pursed her lips. Then she looked up at the unicorn, now floating dangerously close to the edge of the shed. The right gust and it'd be sailing outside.

'Wouldn't take much to lose the lot if the weather turned bad,' I pressed.

She sighed. 'You're right. I'll fill them on the verandah. They can go into the formal dining room. There's nothing in there anyway.'

I carried the gas bottle to the verandah and came back for the boxes. There seemed to be a lot of them, and I wondered how big she was going to make the letters this time. April helped, stacking the boxes in neat piles against the wall of the house.

April insisted on doing the filling, reminding me with a smile that she was the welder on Rainbow, and knew a thing or two about gas. My task was to attach the sticks and keep the balloons together in their species group. The shapes were unwieldy enough on their own, bunched together they were worse. My solution was to create animal barbells: balloon figures at either end, sticks in the middle tied tight.

'So what are the windmills for?' I asked while waiting for a lurid butterfly's wings to inflate.

'You'll see.'

We stopped for a cuppa mid-afternoon, enjoying the warmth of April's kitchen and a packet of chocolate biscuits she opened especially for me. The nervousness about me being in her house had faded and now April seemed comfortable with my presence. She laughed when I rinsed my cup and put it on the drainer until I reminded her that Mum wasn't the sort of woman to tolerate messy boys. Which was why I could not only wash dishes, but iron and feed myself.

'What did I tell you?' she said, winking at me. 'You're too much.'

'Not where it counts.'

I meant it in my heart but it came out like an innuendo. I was too shocked by my mistake to explain.

April kept looking at me, green eyes enormous and swimming with laughter. 'I can't believe you said that.'

'I didn't. I mean . . .' I clamped my mouth shut and tried to calm myself but embarrassment had me in its grip. I pointed down the hall. 'Loo?'

She was still laughing. 'Third on your right.'

I walked off, wanting to crawl. Passing a half open door, I couldn't help glancing inside. A single bed was made up with a quilt printed with an astronaut's body suit, the pillow with a bulbous astronaut's helmet. I thought how fun that would be to sleep in if you were a little boy.

I washed my face, trying to cool it down. When I passed the door on the way back it was closed.

Stupidly, it wasn't until I was lying in bed later that night, thinking of April's teasing eyes and laughter, that I realised what the room meant.

And everything made sense.

SIXTEEN

The morning was perfect, one of those calm winter days with a vivid sunlit sky that appeared so rarely in the western districts, but which reinforced why this was considered God's country by so many locals.

Now that I had April's assurance of financial help, I'd been spending a lot of time at the back of Rainbow, fencing mainly, and planning in my head. I'd talked a lot to Dad and Laurie, and also the district agronomist who had a real passion for erosion management. Most evenings I spent at the kitchen table, working on my plans. I'd ordered satellite photos, and sheets of plastic and marker pens. Each clear sheet represented a stage of rehabilitation, with the work required carefully marked out. When all were layered on top of the satellite photos, the final picture emerged. Rainbow the way it should be.

First task was to fence off the worst areas to stop stock wandering over the fragile soils. After that would come tree planting and pasture renovation using deep-rooted perennials.

Thanks to the conversations we'd had while staring at her Suffolks – now, much to my relief, more dirty pastel than paintbox acrylic – April understood my dedication and insisted that my work come before hers. So it wasn't until after lunch that I wandered up to the main house to help her with PLAY.

A sleek four-door Aston Martin, also red, was parked behind the Range Rover. If I was a car man I probably would have walked closer for a look but cars had never been my thing, and impractical ones like this even less so. It was beautiful though and I bet it went like a cut snake, but cars like this cost stupid amounts of money, and for what? Prestige? So the driver could flaunt their wealth or look like a big man? There were more important things in life.

April had never had a visitor that I was aware of. She'd never mentioned family or friends. In our discussions about art she'd revealed she'd studied at university in Melbourne but not much more. I knew she'd gone to a posh private school. Any idiot could work out she had plenty of money – you don't buy a property like Rainbow for under a couple of million, and her Range Rover wasn't cheap either.

I glanced at the sky and regarded the house, unsure what to do. Perhaps she wouldn't want to be disturbed if she had family visiting, and God knows I wasn't great in company. But today was perfect for PLAY. Tomorrow the wind might get up, the weather might turn, and April said this installation was special. I hoped she meant that it would be the one to give her peace.

The screen door opened with a bang. A man came striding out. April stepped out onto the verandah, her hands clutched low below her belly and wrestling with one another.

The man saw me and faltered, then his stride became even more purposeful as he crossed the yard. I glanced past him to April. She held my gaze, worry crumpling her face.

'You must be Tristan,' he said, hand held out.

I nodded and shook. His grip was firm, and he took my elbow with his other hand. The sort of double-handed greeting that politicians use to get people on side. Distrust surged through me in a wave. This man wasn't April's friend. Which sure as hell meant he wasn't mine.

I couldn't stop looking at her, the defeated way she stood, the downturn of her mouth.

'I'm Sebastian Tremayne.'

I regarded him properly then. Green eyes, dark hair, same nose. Good-looking in a polished, urban way.

'April's brother.'

I knew I should be doing more than nodding but I'd learned a long time ago that silence had a way of drawing people out. The void made them feel awkward and they'd often race to fill it. And I wanted to know what was going on.

'I can see you're worried about her too.'

I returned my gaze to April, trying to reassure her that I could handle this, that I was on her side. 'April's fine.'

He pursed his lips, assessing. 'You've been helping her with her installations?'

'Yes.' He waited for more and I relented. 'She's very talented.'

'She is. Very.' His expression softened. 'My

sister was highly lauded when she was younger.' He held my gaze. 'She's also very fragile, Tristan.'

My jaw clenched at the repeat of my name. I knew what he was doing, trying to make me his mate.

'I want her to come home.'

I said nothing.

'Your job would remain safe, of course.'

I shot him a sharp glance and looked back at April. She was hugging herself and pacing the verandah, her lips moving as though in silent prayer.

'Ah, I see.' Sebastian glanced at April and back to me. 'In that case, if you feel anything for my sister, you'll try to convince her to come home where she can get help.'

'Rainbow's helping her.'

Sebastian shook his head in frustration. 'Rainbow is making her worse.'

Suddenly April jumped off the verandah and sprinted toward us. She skidded on the gravel and I reached out to steady her. Her arm was freezing. I shifted my hand to her back as she thrust her chin out at her brother.

'I want you off here.'

'You need to come home!'

'This is home!'

'For Christ's sake, April. He's not here. He's not anywhere. He's dead!'

'No.' She shook her head, wild hair whipping. 'No.' I could feel the tremble in her body and wanted to hold her. 'It's you who can't see. He's here. He sees me.' She splayed her hand over her chest, her eyes pooling. 'He feels me.'

Sebastian's face caved in and for a moment I thought he was going to start crying. 'Don't do this, April. Please.'

'I'm staying. I found him at Rainbow. I'm never leaving.'

Sebastian drew her against him, his pleading gaze meeting mine over her shoulder. I breathed in hard, stuck between April and the brother who I could now see loved and feared for her. He shook his head and cradled her face to his heart, laying his cheek on her hair.

'Stay safe, sis.' Still holding her, he mouthed 'call me' and reached around April to hold out a business card. His eyes widened, urging me to take it. I shoved it quickly in my pocket, afraid April would see my betrayal.

He let her go, and held her by the shoulders. 'I'll be watching. One more sign, April.' He held up a finger. 'One more and you won't get a choice.'

April pulled away, her voice weary. 'It's my life.'

'Yes, and I want you to live it. But right now you're drowning.' Sebastian sighed and ruffled her hair then threw me another meaningful look before striding to his car.

The engine sounded like a lion. April and I watched the car until it melted into the landscape. She turned and headed for the house, leaving me alone and worried sick. At the verandah, she stopped.

'I don't feel up to PLAY today.'

'Do you need company?'

She sucked on her lip looked toward the horizon. I waited, my guts churning. She shook her head and forced a smile. 'You go. Rainbow needs you.'

'And you don't?'

She blinked, opened her mouth and shut it again.

'I know what you lost,' I said quietly.

'No, Tristan, you don't.' And with that she walked inside and closed the door, abandoning me to the cold while she carried on suffocating herself in private grief.

SEVENTEEN

'He was eight,' said April, her voice hollow. 'In a month it'll be his tenth birthday. Such a beautiful, beautiful boy.'

I took her cold hand and pressed it between mine. The weather had held, and now I sat with April on the verandah with the sun shining on us and April's paddock below. The ground was cleared, ready for an installation that might never be built.

I'd felt sick leaving her the previous day. For an hour after she'd closed the door on me I'd hung around, tinkering in the main shed. A flash of silver had me wandering across to April's shed to see if I could catch the unicorn that still floated around the roof. Catching it was like trying to hold April. The moment I thought I had it safe it jerked out of reach. My temper flared with each failed attempt until I gave it up. Eventually, I did the same with April.

Except not in my heart.

I walked back to the cottage, fingering Sebastian's card, tossing up whether to call. His worry had been genuine, and after April's reaction to his pleas I could easily sympathise with his need to get her somewhere safe. But the way she'd spoken about her son, the passion in her words, the love, how she would never leave Rainbow now she'd discovered him here, made me hesitant.

Who was I to tell her how to grieve? Who was anyone?

I hid Sebastian's card in my sock drawer and went back to work. Somehow I'd find a way to help April be happy again. But I think that even then I knew she never would be, that Rainbow would never produce a fairytale ending. And I was going to be more hurt than I'd ever been in my life.

The next day I found her on the verandah as dawn broke over the hills, as unable to sleep as I was. She was wearing her multi-coloured skirt and emerald parka again, teamed with her yellow rubber boots. Her hair was out but she'd used some sort of dye to line it with rainbow stripes. Her skin was pale, her hands mottled from the cold, or perhaps a heart too weak with grief to pump blood into her fingertips.

'What was his name?'

She smiled wistfully. 'Daniel. Daniel Arthur Tremayne. My darling boy.'

Tremayne, like Sebastian. Her name and not the father's.

A tear began its slow trickle down her cheek. 'He was so precious. So very, very precious.' She looked down. 'Being young, we were nervous parents and looked out for him constantly, but he was still a little boy, with a little boy's sense of adventure and embrace of life. We knew that depriving him of that, making him scared of the world instead of wide-eyed with its wonders, would have been wrong.'

A magpie warbled and she looked up, a wondrous look on her face, as though the call was some sort of sign that Daniel was listening. My mind sped to the card in my sock drawer. I tightened my jaw.

'He was on an overnight camping trip to the Dandenong Ranges. It was his first away from us and our constant supervision, and he was so excited. As we were for him, our little growing boy. It should have been safe. He should have come home as beautiful and perfect as he left, but the campground was surrounded by trees. One dropped a branch in the night.' She pulled her hand from mine and buried her face in her palms, sobbing.

I wrapped my arm around her and drew her close, letting her cry herself out, knowing that even when her tears dried, inside they would continue to fall without end.

Finally she sniffed and sat back straight, staring at the paddock.

I fidgeted, desperate to ask the question that burned so fiercely inside me, hating myself for my selfishness. 'Daniel's dad . . .' I couldn't go on.

April let out a noise somewhere between a sneer and a laugh. 'Daniel's father disappeared overseas to,' she held up fingers and made air quotes, '"find himself" two months after the funeral. When he finally came back he said he was better now.' She shook her head. 'How I hated him for that. How could anything be better with Daniel gone?'

We sat for a while, watching the day emerge.

'He's nothing like you,' said April.

I frowned, thinking she meant Daniel.

'He's an artist too. A painter, a very good one. Successful.' She sounded begrudging. 'He wants to get back together.'

I stilled.

She looked at me in a way that told me she knew what I was feeling. 'He left me, Tristan. Ran away overseas when I needed him most. When every breath, every waking moment was agony. Do you really think I want a man like that in my life?'

I shook my head while inside I was imagining the tortures I'd make him suffer if I ever came close to the bastard. I held her gaze. 'I would never have left you.'

She sighed and tilted her head to rest it on my shoulder. 'Yes, but you're honourable, like your namesake.'

I knew the story, of course. Tristan and Isolde, famous lovers like Romeo and Juliet. Tristan was a Cornish knight; brave, honest and tormented by the love he felt for the wife of his uncle, who was also his king and a man Tristan admired deeply. In the end, he was doomed by his own desire.

'I hope not. I wouldn't call shagging your uncle's wife honourable.'

She laughed a little. 'He couldn't help it, he loved her. He loved them both.'

'Yeah, and in the end it killed him.'

'Ah, but that depends on which legend you believe. One version has him going off to France and marrying another Isolde.'

I hmphed. 'Then he's an even bigger idiot than I thought.'

'That's a bit black and white.'

I shrugged. 'He loved her. He should have stayed.'

'And suffered for it?'

I brought her closer to me until she was cradled under my arm. 'He would have suffered even more by being away from her.' I kissed her hair. 'Are you going to build PLAY?'

'Yes.'

I curled my head to meet her eye. 'Should we get on with it?'

'I guess we should.' She began to ease away from me.

'April?'

'What?'

'You'll tell me, won't you? If you need help?'

She smiled and stroked her hand affectionately over my head as she stepped up onto the verandah, then kept walking, leaving me without an answer.

I sat for a while, thinking about what had just happened, what it all meant. I'd held her hand, cradled her to my side, kissed her hair, talked about love, and not once had I felt the itchy crawl of heat up my neck that had spoiled so many other of my encounters with April.

She was making me better.

I wished I could do the same for her.

I found her in the dining room where the balloons were stacked like a fantastical creatures' lair. She had a round of wire and cutters, and was threading the wire through holes in the ends of the plastic poles fixed to the balloons. From a box she picked out a heavy metal disc with a large hole in the centre, and threaded it onto the wire before twisting the loop closed.

I hadn't noticed the holes in the plastic poles but now I saw what she was doing it seemed an obvious solution.

'What are they? Sinkers?'

'Weight plates, like what you use on dumbbells.'

'Not something I've ever needed.'

'No.' Her gaze flicked over my body in a way that made me feel hot. 'You have manlier ways of keeping in shape.'

Manlier. I liked that but I liked her lingering gaze more.

April only had one pair of wire cutters so I jogged back to the cottage for another pair, returning in the ute, which we'd need to carry everything down to the paddock anyway. We spent the morning fixing wires, talking. She talked about artists like Brancusi and Rodin, and the influence they had on her work when she was young, before she found her own direction. I talked about old man McKenna and how sad I felt that his property was being fought over.

A cosiness developed between us. Sometimes I'd look up after threading a wire and find her watching me. Not with a smile on her face but something else. Our eyes would lock, and I'd have to force myself to stay seated when what I really wanted to do was press my lips against hers and breathe every drop of her sadness into me until she was happy again.

Within a few hours all the balloons had weights and my fingers ached from the fiddly work. April and I took our cups of tea outside to the verandah where she explained to me how she wanted the design to work. To my relief, PLAY would be smaller than HAPPY, but what it lacked it size it would make up for in sparkle.

'Like sideshow alley condensed into a tiny space.' April was standing, excited. 'Small, but unable to hide its glittery glory.' She spread her arms to the sky. 'An invitation.'

From a heartbroken mother to a son who would never play in this world again.

God, I ached for her.

I left her to her twirling and carried the cups inside. Her smartphone sat on the kitchen bench and I thought again of Sebastian's card, of his pleading gaze. The fear he felt for his sister.

I glanced out the window and my own anxiety lurched hard as April continued to twirl, eyes closed and arms wide, her skirt and hair flashing with colour.

And in that moment I realised I was like the other Tristan.

Damned by my own love.

EIGHTEEN

We finished PLAY just before sunset. April insisted on walking over to the cairn to watch it as the sun flashed its last rays.

There was no question PLAY was glorious. It sparkled and moved like an overloaded Christmas tree, except somehow happier. At first it was only the word that caught my eye, then I began to pick the bob of individual animals. On every sweep of breeze, the little sparkly windmills whirled and flashed even more sparkles.

We sat on the blanket, holding hands, until the sun dropped completely and PLAY became a smear in the dark.

I regarded April with a mixture of awe and admiration and heart-pounding adoration. 'It's beautiful.' I squeezed her hand. 'Like you.'

She smiled back at me and I caught another of those looks that made my heart flutter and fill.

I stood and held out my hand. 'Come on. It's getting cold.'

Obsession pinched her face. She refocused on PLAY. 'I want to stay. Watch it in the moonlight.'

'No.'

'But he's here. I can feel him.'

I closed my eyes and thought of Sebastian's card. When I opened them, April's expression had become one of panic.

I knelt in front of her, blocking her view. 'He'll still be here tomorrow.'

Her lip trembled.

'Please, April. You're no good to Daniel if you get sick.' I rubbed her upper arm, hating myself for playing along with her delusion but not knowing what else to do. 'What about all the other things you have planned for him? How will you get those done?'

I had no knowledge of any of April's plans but I understood enough to know she wouldn't leave his forthcoming birthday uncelebrated.

'I hate leaving him.'

'You're not. How can you if you're still at Rainbow?' I took her hand and tugged. 'Come on. I have a casserole at the cottage. You can share it with me.'

But when we arrived back at the house she refused to come along, standing on the verandah shivering and shaking her head when I tried to change her mind.

So I asked if I could stay instead.

I was on the lawn, April on the raised verandah, our heads at the same height. Suddenly she cupped my face and pressed her forehead against mine. Her breath caressed my lips. I closed my eyes and tilted slightly, wanting to catch her mouth.

'Tristan.'

I opened my lids.

'It won't help.'

I nuzzled her, whispering over the pound of my

heart. 'You don't know that.' I kissed her cheek, her neck. She moaned softly and the pound became canon fire.

'Please, Tristan.' It wasn't a plea for more.

For two long breaths I pressed into the silky skin of her neck then took a step back and shoved my hands deep into my pockets. I tilted my head and stared at the stars beginning to wink into life.

Idiot. Idiot. Idiot.

I looked at her, horrified to see tears in her eyes. Tears my selfish stupidity had caused. 'I'm sorry. I'll go.' I turned toward the ute and then spun back. 'Promise me you won't go back there.'

She hesitated and nodded.

'Say it.'

'I promise.'

I blew out a breath and watched the steam fade into the night. 'Thank you.' I locked my gaze with hers, the words I wanted so desperately to say forming in my head. I willed them to my lips but they wouldn't come.

'I'll be back at dawn to take you over.'

'You don't have to. I can walk.'

'I want to. I want to do everything for you.'

She smiled sadly, as if she wasn't worth it. But she was. She was worth the moon and the stars and the sun and the earth and every comet and meteor and tiny planet in the universe and beyond.

'Goodnight, Tristan.'

'Goodnight, April.'

I lingered until she was inside before walking on.

As promised, I was there the following morning, Holly by my side, watching the sun shoot exploratory rays across the hills as I waited. The screen door creaked open and April smiled at me as if nothing had happened in last night's darkness. As if there was nothing to forgive.

But I had my speech and I was determined to say it.

She frowned at me as she pulled on her boots. 'You look tired.'

I had my hat in my hands and was rolling the brim. 'Last night. I'm sorry.'

'What for?'

'For forcing myself on you. For . . .' I searched for the right word as baboon's bum began its itchy creep. That it was back only added to my misery, which was deep and dark enough already. I made myself keep my head up even though all I wanted was to look at my boots. 'For being an idiot.'

'You're not an idiot, Tristan. And you didn't force yourself on me.'

I clamped my mouth shut before I made things worse.

She came down the steps, pausing to pat Holly, before continuing on to me. 'Did you stew over this all night?'

'That, and worrying you'd go across the road.'

'I promised you I wouldn't.'

'I know but . . .'

'But you didn't trust me.' She sighed. 'You were probably right not to. I thought about it.' She slid a smile at me. 'But I stayed inside.'

I let out my breath.

She kept looking at me as I drove her to the cairn.

'What?' I asked, when I could stand it no longer.

'Nothing.'

I pulled up near the edge of the grassed area and turned off the engine. 'Sure?'

She unclicked her seatbelt and twisted to face me, her elbow on the back of the seat and her head resting in the palm of her hand.

I let out a nervous laugh. 'Okay, what?'

'I want you to listen to me.'

I flexed my hands around the steering wheel. 'I always listen to you.'

'Yes, but this time I want you to believe it.' She pressed her other hand against my heart. 'In there.'

I cleared my throat and slid my hands down the front legs of my jeans.

'Look at me.'

I did, and wanted to cry from the honesty in her face.

'You're the one who's beautiful, Tristan. Inside, outside, all over. You're not and never have been an idiot around me. You've been kind and gentle and caring and clever and sweet.'

My mouth parted.

'And don't you dare think otherwise, okay?'

I nodded, too choked up to speak anyway.

'Good. Now that we have that sorted I'm going to talk with my son.' She opened the door. 'Oh, and one other thing.'

I looked at her.

Her jaw jutted. 'No matter what my brother says, I'm not crazy.'

Oh, but she was. Crazy, depressed, manic, grieving, obsessed. But I think, even overcrowded as she was with all that, somewhere inside there, curled up in a tight secret corner, existed a little bit of love for me.

NINETEEN

PLAY lasted four days before the balloons became too deflated to be attractive and the windmills had lost too many of their shiny twirlers to be special any more.

The following week I tagged along with Dad and Jeremy to the local saleyards and spent most of the time with my jaw clenched. Chuckles and snide comments followed me like a bad wind. A few were just teases but some weren't. The ones about polluting the landscape with fairground rubbish and wool clips with tainted wool held an edge of snarl that signalled the ill-will behind them.

Afraid of what would come out of my mouth, I spoke even less than usual. Dad filled in the gaps. Jeremy made jokes to cover the fury curdling off me. I stalked and glared, trying to keep a stopper on my temper. Locals I'd known for years eyed me with surprise and curiosity.

If the men were bad, the wives were harder. April was new to the area, young and beautiful, but on those few times she'd ventured into town her fragility had been noted. As had her vigils below the cairn. Their concern was genuine. Their expressions kind as they cornered me and enquired if Ms Tremayne was okay. If she needed any womanly help, or if perhaps she would be amenable to joining them for a cuppa and cake one day. I controlled my temper enough to mumble something about Mum keeping an eye on things, before escaping as fast as I could.

I think every one of them knew how I felt about April. Trouble was, I could see from their pitying expressions that every one of them also thought that it was hopeless. A woman like her with a bloke like me? No chance. But they didn't know her. They hadn't seen us together, the way April sometimes looked at me.

Despite PLAY going out of action, April's mood seemed high. We spent a fun morning popping the remaining balloons and packing the rubbish into the leftover cartons. The wire April kept for recycling, the same with the weights. I'd been tossing them into a pile and she kept stopping by to study it with her finger pressed against her mouth. I could almost see her mind spinning with future ideas for them and felt warmed. Thinking ahead could only signal something positive, or so I fooled myself into believing.

The only downer on the day was a carload of dickheads who kept hooning up and down the road, blowing the horn and yelling abuse. When they dared pull up at the side of the road, I stood for a moment, watching, and then strode straight toward them with a gaze as cold and inhospitable as Antarctica. They kept on mouthing off until I climbed through the fence and pulled the wire cutters from my back pocket.

The one in the rear – a teenage boy, not a man,

and closest to me – began to bang on the back of the seat in front, yelling for the others to go, go, go. They laughed until the first blow landed and shattered the rear windscreen. I received a mouthful of abuse but their tyres skidded until they found traction and they were off. I stood with my fists rested on my hips and my legs apart in a 'you're messing with the wrong bloke' stance, until I was certain they wouldn't be returning. Then I ducked through the fence and jogged back to April.

She was on her bum, arms clutched around her belly, laughing herself stupid. 'Oh, Tristan, you should have seen yourself.'

'Impressed?'

She nodded with her mouth closed, but little giggles kept bubbling up until she burst out laughing again. Enchanted by her joy and the admiration glittering her eyes, I could only manage to stare in wonder and hope.

'Come here,' she said, finally, crooking her finger at me. I eased down beside her while Holly watched with her head cocked. Her curled finger turned into a curled palm as she slid it behind my neck, and drew me to her. Her lips touched mine too briefly. 'You are amazing.'

'It's all you.' I wanted her to kiss me again but I'd learned my lesson about forcing myself on her. 'I wasn't like this until I met you.'

She hadn't moved her hand, our mouths were only centimetres apart. I was too confused by her to know whether to bridge the space or not and, burnt, I erred on the side of caution.

'Is this a good or bad thing?' she asked.

'Good. With you there's only good.'

April sighed and closed her eyes, her expression almost beatific, like she'd just witnessed a miracle or encountered a sex-god rock star. My chest felt as though my ribs couldn't hold my elation.

'April?'

She opened her eyes.

'You make me the man I want to be.'

April began to cry.

I gathered her to me. 'I'm sorry. I'm sorry. I didn't mean it. I didn't.'

She slapped at my chest. 'Don't you dare take that away. Don't you dare!'

'Okay, I won't. Shh. Shh.' I rocked her, my anxiety worsening as I came down from my adrenalin rush. 'Come on,' I said when the worst of her sobs had abated. 'You're tired. It's been a big week. You need a lie-down.'

She sniffed and nodded and I helped her to her feet. 'I can carry you, if you want.'

April rewarded me with a watery smile. 'Thanks. But I can walk.'

I kept my arm around her all the way to the house, the proprietary pleasure of it giving me a flush of pride. I sat her in the kitchen and made tea for us both while April blew her nose and settled herself down.

'You smashed their window, you realise that, don't you?'

'It's muddy there, at the edge of the paddock. Easy spot to get bogged. I'd gone down to warn them and slipped. The cutters just happened to go through their rear window.' I quirked one side of my mouth. 'Accident. Could happen to anyone.'

'Tristan Blake, did you just invent a big fat lie?'

I placed my hand on my chest. 'Me?'

She tsked. 'And there I was thinking you were pure of heart.'

I turned back to the cups, adding milk and stirring. 'I am, when it comes to you.'

April didn't respond. I stayed with my back to her, stirring in sugar for longer than necessary while inwardly muttering 'idiot' to myself.

Hands slid around my waist. April's head rested against my back. Unsure, I stiffened, then carefully put the spoon down and twisted in her hold until I faced her.

I stroked her hair, still dyed in rainbow stripes. 'Are you okay?'

She lifted her face and searched mine. I didn't move. I wasn't going to spoil this. If April wanted to make a move or if she pulled away, I'd accept whatever her decision was.

'Tristan?'

'What?'

'Will you kiss me?'

I stroked her hair again, pushing the silken strands away from her forehead, stalling.

'You don't want to?'

'You know I do.'

'So?'

What was I meant to say? That she made my gut churn with as much anxiety as it did love? That I was worried she'd be kissing me not because she loved me, but because I loved her so pathetically she felt obliged? That I wanted to, desperately, but I was afraid she'd make me stop again and I'd feel like dying at her feet because I'd somehow hurt her, when I never wanted to hurt her ever?

'April . . .' I let out a breath. 'Do you really want this?'

She closed her eyes.

I bent and kissed her forehead, holding my lips there. 'It's okay.'

She fisted hunks of my jumper and let out a growl, before thrusting away and slumping down at the table to wrap her hands into her hair instead.

I followed and grabbed her hands, disentangled her fingers and curled them open until I could place a kiss on each palm. I smiled at her. 'That I can do this is enough.'

While April rested, I spent the rest of the day clearing the paddock of the remaining scraps of PLAY, thinking about what had happened.

Things were changing between us, that much was clear. Intensifying. The love that I only suspected April harboured for me was trying to break through.

I just had to be man enough to hold back and not scare it off.

TWENTY

After PLAY, April took to joining me around the farm. She always carried a sketchbook, a large one that covered her lap and was filled with thickish card. Mostly she sketched the farm and Holly, using charcoal that left her hands black and cute smears on her face.

One day in the ute, as I pulled in to drop her back at the house, she flicked through her book until she found the sheet she wanted and broke it free from the binding. A sweet pink flush coloured her cheeks when she handed it over.

I could only blink at what she'd drawn.

She'd given me a couple of sketches of Holly already, which I'd had framed and now stood proudly on the cottage's mantel, but this was the first time that I knew she'd sketched me. It wasn't a likeness in the perfect sense. As she'd explained before, April wasn't a realist artist. Her work was abstract, using imagery to capture the essence of her subject.

But I had never been more recognisable.

With planes and thick lines, shadows and hollows and stripes of movement, she'd caught me. Not the me I saw in the mirror, but me as I thought I was. Solid, dependable, big, steadfast. I was fencing, that much was clear, Holly nearby.

But April made it seem like I was building a new world.

I swallowed, suddenly afraid I'd say the wrong thing. The paper shook and I willed myself to steadiness.

'Tristan?'

'I can't...' I looked at her. 'I can't find the words.'

She smiled. 'And that's news?'

I made an effort to sort my jumbled thoughts. 'You see me.' I screwed up my nose. 'Not me.' I breathed out hard, frustrated. 'The way I see my spirit.' Feeling foolish, I turned away.

'Really?'

Confused by the delight in her voice, I faced her again. 'Yes.'

She let out a sigh. 'You say the best things.'

I grinned my relief. 'I try.'

She matched my grin and I felt her unspoken encouragement for me to take to chance and kiss her. Instead I lowered my face to study the sketch once more. Out of the corner of my eye I caught the sag of disappointment in her face and hated myself for it.

And then I made it worse.

'Have you spoken to Sebastian lately?'

'Why?'

'Just asking.'

'Has he called you? What did he say?' Panic made her hands flutter.

I grabbed them. 'Nothing, nothing. Forget I mentioned it. He hasn't called. I haven't called him. I was just asking.'

'No. No. You wouldn't have mentioned it without a reason.' She snatched her hands away and swung open the ute door.

'April, please.'

Her breathing was rapid, her eyes huge. 'He's poisoning you, isn't he?'

'What? No.' I reached for her but she was gone. I pushed my own door open. She was scurrying to the house with her sketchpad clutched to her chest. 'April!'

The door slammed. I stood there, flummoxed. I pulled my hat off to scratch my head, not understanding what the hell had just happened, how I could have screwed things up so fast with one simple question.

I looked at Holly, who glanced at the house and then back at me. 'Yeah, I know.'

But still I didn't move. I looked instead at the sky, at the thick clouds with their nasty bellies threatening rain. The weather was about to do one of its usual somersaults and turn sunshine to ice and the soil to mud. The long range forecast wasn't good either. I'd been watching it, not just for myself but for April, with one date in mind: Daniel's tenth birthday.

Holly's whine sent me into action. I knocked, not expecting an answer nor getting one. I kept calling as I pushed open the door, trying to keep my voice neutral.

With still no answer and a last glance at Holly I entered and closed the door behind me. The house was quiet, not even a tap drip, tick-tock of a clock, or a groan of timber to give it life.

'April?'

I walked to the kitchen and glanced around, but the room was empty. I took a deep breath and girded myself for Daniel's room. The door was ajar. I pushed it carefully open but it, too, was empty.

Anxiety began to churn harder. 'April?'

I passed the bathroom, also empty. The door of the next room was closed. I tapped lightly. 'April?'

Something muffled sounded inside.

I looked down the hall to the main door and back at the barrier in front of me. It was just a bedroom door, but it felt like it had the weight and solidity of a bank vault.

'I'm coming in.'

I turned the knob and pushed the door open. April lay on her side on a large timber-framed bed. The sketchbook was on the floor. She'd pulled the doona around her so she lay half-wrapped it in, rather than under.

'April?'

'Go away.'

'No.'

'I want to be alone.'

I took a few steps into the room. 'I don't.' I swallowed. 'I don't ever want to be alone from you.'

A muffled sob sounded.

'I'm not on anyone's side except yours. You know that.' I approached the bed and knelt down on the floor beside it until I was face to face with the woman I loved. I rested my chin on the bed, centimetres from hers. 'I know you're scared but please don't do this. Don't question what you know is true.'

She squeezed her eyes shut and rolled onto her back away from me, palm spread over her face to cover most of her expression. But her mouth was so screwed up I knew she was in terrible pain.

'April?'

She sobbed.

'Can I lie next to you?'

She nodded fast.

I stood and made my way to the other side of the bed, and took a moment to untangle the doona until it was still over April but I was on top of it. A chastity belt of duck down. I dug for her hand and gripped it firmly.

We lay for a long time, me staring at the ceiling trying to work out what to do, April restless, as if she didn't know what to do either. We were in her bedroom, on her bed, and I wanted her like she'd burrowed her hand through my ribcage and wrapped her fingers around my heart to tug it toward her.

'Daniel's birthday is in three weeks,' she said.

'I know. It must hurt.'

'Yes.'

We lapsed back into silence. There was nothing else to add to that.

'Tristan?'

'What?'

'It might make it better.'

I shut my eyes and listened to her shuffle free of the quilt. She was above me, kneeling. Her hand traced across my forehead. She lowered her body until it was alongside mine, until she rested on her elbow, her upper body curled over my shoulder.

I couldn't pretend any longer that she wasn't there, that it wasn't her making the move. I opened my eyes and caught a tress of her beautiful rainbow hair in my hand, pulling the strands away and letting them fall back in a cascade of silk.

She leaned closer until I could feel her breath on mine. My heart fluttered, I felt sick and elated and scared all at the same time.

Just a kiss, I promised myself. Just a kiss and no more, and then I'd go home and let her sleep her distress away.

Her lips touched mine. Hesitant then stronger. My hand fell from her hair and slipped to her shoulder and back as the kiss shifted from experimental and careful to special and impassioned.

'April,' I whispered, kissing her cheek, her neck, nibbling her ear, kissing back down to her collarbone as she arched beneath me.

And then her hands found my hot skin and I was gone, lost in a place more fantastic than any of April's balloon animals could ever create.

So warm, so full of her, of everything, that I never wanted to leave.

TWENTY-ONE

That afternoon triggered something in April. She sparkled and glowed and danced and laughed and, stupid-happy, I glowed and danced and laughed alongside her.

As anticipated, the weather turned. Rain lashed Rainbow and left it sodden and ice-cold. I moved all the sheep to the most sheltered paddocks, where the slopes and remnant forest protected them from the slicing wind. I watched the creek and the trees, and checked the erosion-prone slopes for slippage, Holly beside me.

And on my return to the house I'd hunt down April and slide my hands over her warm skin and kiss her neck and believe I was the most blessed human on earth.

During the worst of the rain she remained inside, sliding her finger across the screen of her tablet computer, making notes. Sometimes she sketched, other times I found her lying on Daniel's bed, very still and straight, clutching one of his toys to her chest as though she'd been laid out for a coffin. I'd walk softly away, leaving her, while my heart would hammer and my stomach would clench, and my mind would find itself drifting to my sock drawer and Sebastian's card.

Whenever the weather relented and a clear

patch formed, April would dash outside to her paddock. She'd step out measurements, pausing often with her finger pressed to her lips. Sometimes I'd catch her not doing anything, just staring at the horizon with a vacant expression, having drifted off with Daniel.

A week passed. At night I held her spooned against me, my lips on her shoulder and neck, wanting this to last forever, loving her so badly I was nothing but a torrent of yearning and fear.

I guessed that's how the original Tristan felt about his Isolde, except for me I wasn't sharing April with my uncle the king, I was sharing her with a dead child who would forever hold more of April's love than I ever could.

One Saturday, when I'd been at footy getting belted around and hailed on, I came home to find April in the front paddock. She was wearing her coloured skirt and a bright orange wool jumper and no coat or hat or gloves. Her only concession to the filthy rain was her rubber boots. She was soaked, but carrying on with her work, using a spade to mark lines the grass, as though she had no idea that it was raining.

Powered only by panic, I sprinted down to her. I snatched away the spade and threw it down and shook her by the shoulders. 'What are you doing?'

'Tristan!' She kissed me hard on the mouth then pulled away, twirling. 'It's going to be beautiful!'

I wanted to cry. I wanted to snatch her up and hide her forever.

'April, you need to come inside.'

She shook her head. 'No, no. He's here.'

I scraped my hand over my head. The words 'he's not and never will be' rang through my mind. 'Come with me. He'll still be here when the rain stops.'

Her eyes were full of delusion.

'You can finish it tomorrow. The Bureau's forecasting the front will move through by lunch. We can come back out then.' I held out my hand for her, pretending this was all normal.

Finally, she skipped my way and joined her frozen fingers with mine. We walked back to the house as if the sun was shining and the wind calm and the temperature was thirty degrees instead of ten.

I put her in the shower and left her to get warm while I stoked the fire she'd let burn down in my absence. The table was covered in sketches and maths calculations. I didn't want to look at this other sign of her troubled mind. I sat on my haunches in front of the fire and stared at the flickering flames while my body ached from cold and footy, and the heartsickness that had lodged like a fat slug inside.

April came out wearing a thick dressing gown and bright pink ugg boots. Her hair was wet and straggly around her face. She shuffled toward me and pressed her palm onto the back of my neck. I looked up at her, relieved to see from her wan smile that her mania had passed.

'How are you feeling?'

She shrugged and stared at the work she'd left on the table.

'I'll make you a cuppa.'

She stroked my hair. 'You should shower too.'

'I can wait. Why don't you sit down in front of the fire and stay warm?'

She hugged herself, swaying.

'April,' I said, rising and holding her to me, 'it's okay. I'm here.'

'I'm not crazy. I'm not.'

'I know.' I kissed her wet hair, stroked her spine.

'I'm scared, Tristan.'

'Don't be. I'm here. I won't let anything hurt you.'

'Promise you won't abandon me? No matter what.'

'I promise. You're safe with me, I swear.'

She seemed to soften then and I wondered if Daniel's father knew of the scars he'd left behind when he'd selfishly gone off to 'find himself'. He had to be a complete ignoramus if he thought he could get her back after what he'd done. Not only that, but a fool for leaving her in the first place. She might be fragile and grieving but April was still the most beautiful, clever, sexy and sweet-hearted woman I'd ever encountered.

April stayed quiet that evening. She curled up on the sofa with a book while I pretended to watch telly and read *The Weekly Times*. I was observing her though, out of the corner of my eye, and sometimes blatantly. Taking in her face, her hair, her hands, the way she could tuck herself like a question mark into the corner of the couch. I kept thinking of her mouth and skin, the tenderness of her kisses, the way her body glided like satin against mine.

She was the most precious thing I would ever have in my life and I couldn't have loved her more.

She placed her book on the coffee table and leaned her head back, eyeing me. 'You should stop looking at me like that and take me to bed instead.'

I never needed to be told twice. The telly went off. I bent over April and kissed her, then gathered her up in my arms, lifting her as though she was a doll. While I carried her to the bedroom, she nuzzled my neck and whispered sexy talk into my ear, knowing from experience what it did to me. And what I'd do to her in return.

The next few days passed fine but I remained anxious, glancing often at the calendar pinned to the fridge door. The date that April had drawn a rainbow over shimmered with menace as though it were alive.

Worried, I tried to talk to her about her plans for Daniel's birthday.

'Let me keep my secret a little longer,' she said, then kissed me in a way that fuddled my brain and made me useless for anything but kissing her back. 'You can help when the time comes.'

It was another word installation, I'd guessed that from the sketches I'd seen, and I was foolish enough to hope that April's special word would be for both me and Daniel. The same word I had yet to say to her, but had shouted with every kiss, every caress, every look, every action, thought and breath I owned.

I was going to tell her, after Daniel's birthday, and I was going to ask other words, too. Make the ultimate promise, the one only our deaths would ever part.

But first April had to create LOVE.

TWENTY-TWO

Three days before Daniel's birthday vans started turning up at Rainbow. They were dark green, embellished with fancy gold lettering announcing they were from Hanford's Horticulture. April's Range Rover was moved from its bay and her entire shed cleared. Tall trolley racks were wheeled inside, each containing layers of plants budding with early spring flowers in every colour of the spectrum.

April kept clapping her hands and grinning, circling the racks and caressing leaves and petals while I brooded about the weather and the obsessive burn that threatened to sweep away the woman I loved.

The plants had to be worth thousands, cultivated in nursery conditions with expert horticulturalists tending their every bud, and April was about to plant them out into a common farm paddock. Spring was only a week away but it was still winter. While I felt passionately about the region, the western districts produced weather that could challenge even the hardiest of locals.

I'd already used a whipper snipper to slash the pasture around where April planned to site LOVE, and scraped away the top layer of plant matter to expose the dark loam beneath. After watching

April attempting to turn the rain-heavy soil over on her own, I borrowed a rotary hoe to dig out the letters and spent an afternoon covered in mud and sweat, and swearing under my breath. She worked as hard as me that week, raking and clearing any remaining root clumps until the dirt was smooth and LOVE was stencilled in brown across the slope.

I'd kissed her breathless at the end, when everything was packed away and we could finally rest and admire our handiwork. For a moment, after I'd released her, I thought I saw the word reflected in her eyes. My heart soared, then plummeted when her gaze lost focus and turned inward as she stared into the sky, listening for her son.

When the last van left, April danced toward me, hands making twinkle stars beside her head and her grin wide.

'It's going to be so wonderful, Tristan.' She twirled. 'So, so wonderful!'

I caught her grip and spun her so her back was to my chest and my arms locked around her. I kissed and nuzzled her neck and nipped at her earlobe in that way she liked, reminding her I was alive and here, and not an untouchable spirit.

'How long will it take to plant them out?' I asked.

'A while I imagine. But by dawn on Friday they'll be in, even if I have to keep at it all night.'

I turned to rest my cheek on the top of her head, my eyes closed against the fierceness in her voice. 'It won't come to that.' I'd make damn sure of it. There wasn't a chance in hell I'd let her stay out all night. It was a miracle she'd survived the winter without coming down with pneumonia as it was. 'We'll start after lunch.'

April twisted in my arms until she faced me. Her hand cupped my jaw. 'You are so good to me.'

I wanted to tell her then that it was because I loved her, that it was because I wanted to protect her. That without her, the world lost its colour. But like so much else it remained unsaid. Another moment lost, never to be regained.

She placed a light kiss on my mouth. 'I think Daniel would have liked you.'

I think I would have liked him too. He was part of her, created from her genes and moulded by her personality. But I admit there were times when I thought of Daniel with resentment. Mostly I was sorry and grateful at the same time. If Daniel was still alive April wouldn't be here. She'd be in Melbourne with Daniel's father and I'd be somewhere else, oblivious that my life was hollow and grey because she wasn't in it. He was gone though, leaving April consumed by grief and me consumed by love.

In answer I kissed her, hard and long, my hands teasing her in secret places, exciting her, exciting me, until we had to dash, laughing, to the big shed where I'd broken apart a couple of straw bales for such emergencies.

I think I loved those moments most, when we made love outside. The spontaneity of it. The feeling that we were just a normal couple having fun and loving one another in the most natural way of all. It was earthy and elemental and made Rainbow feel like a real home.

I'd hoped April would sleep for a bit afterward, that I'd get to cradle her and watch her while her face was relaxed and at peace, free from her grief. Free from the mania that seemed to worsen each day and made me churn with fear for my precious, beautiful, damaged April.

She stretched lazily and regarded me through half-lowered lids. 'You sure know how to show a girl a good time, Mr Blake.'

'I do my best, Ms Tremayne.'

She grinned and my heart took a tumble-turn. Then her gaze flicked to the yard and her grin turned to wonder. 'Look, Tristan!' She pointed, excitement radiating off her. 'Look!'

A hawk was circling over the yard, head down, intent on the prey it had spotted. Likely a mouse hiding in the grass, but to April it was a sign.

She scrambled to her feet, her skirt falling back around her ankles, straw in her hair, her breasts uncovered, arm held out, finger following the path of the hawk. A mythological woman with fire in her gaze.

Her hand dropped. 'We need to start now. He's waiting.' Without bothering to do up the buttons of her shirt, she snatched up her jumper, tugged it over her head and scampered off, leaving me to scramble into my jeans and curse under my breath.

She'd left her knickers behind. And her bra. I gathered them both up and strode after her. Calm was needed. I knew from experience that mundane things tended to refocus her mind, like showers and cooking, or a play session with Holly.

'The tractor or ute?' she asked when I approached.

'I'll sort that. How about you have a quick shower and put on some proper work clothes?'

'Oh, no. No time. Daniel's waiting.'

'April, you're not wearing any underwear.' I waved her clothes but she didn't seem to hear. 'You really think your son wants to see his mother out in a paddock without a bra and knickers?'

April began to giggle.

I waggled the knickers. 'Come on, before I stick my hand up your skirt and get dirty again.'

She wouldn't budge. She was going to stomp around a paddock in full view of the road in an impractical skirt, with her clothes half done up and no bra or knickers. Some men might have viewed it in another way, like a giant tease, having to work alongside a woman so easily accessed. I just felt sick with worry.

I considered playing the Neanderthal and carrying her inside. God knows I'd done that enough already, but something inside me told me it would be a mistake, that she wouldn't see it as fun. That she'd fight me. I'd be keeping her from her child and I knew enough about a mother's love to understand how savage it could be when threatened.

April began to hum a tune. "Somewhere over the Rainbow".

My mind flitted to my sock drawer and Sebastian's card.

TWENTY-THREE

Sometimes I think it was April's enthusiasm for LOVE that proved her downfall. In the end though, it was only me.

We finished planting out the flowers early Thursday afternoon. From the cairn the word stood out like a beacon of pure happiness, lighting the world with its colour and sentiment. Cars slowed as they passed. Quite a few took the road to the cairn and pulled up, spilling amazed passengers. Hundreds of photos were taken. People gasped and speculated. Why was LOVE there? Was it for them? Was it a proposal, perhaps, from some lovesick farmer?

I stayed with April, holding her hand while she sat with a funny secretive smile on her face, lost in silent communication with a little boy I couldn't see or hear, but who was stealing April's mind from me. She didn't answer the people who approached and tried to engage her in conversation. Most of the locals took the hint when I shook my head, and backed away. To others I lied and said we were just admiring the view like them.

There was no stopping it. Word would spread and come evening I'd be subject to the usual barrage of phone calls from Mum, Andrea and others. No doubt the paper would send out a photographer again. Somehow, amongst it all, I would have to keep April safe.

At dark we walked back to the house. I talked about anything I could think of that wasn't to do with LOVE or Daniel or even Rainbow. I talked about football and the upcoming agricultural show, and how everyone feared that this would be the last year Rannoch would hold it. Mundane things, anything that might draw April out, but she remained trapped in her separate world. Out of reach.

The irony of it wasn't lost on me. Somehow our roles had been reversed. Now she was the silent one, the one who couldn't find words, and I was the one who talked.

We spent a quiet night. As soon as we were back at the house April refused my pleas to shower and took herself off to Daniel's room. She laid in her death pose on his bed in her filthy skirt and top, clutching his favourite action man toy with dirt-crusted hands, her fingernails thick with grime.

I sat at the kitchen table with my head in my hands, praying that Daniel's birthday tomorrow would bring some kind of peace for April. I wasn't sure for how much longer I'd be able to keep pretending that everything was all right. That my love was enough to vanquish the grief that seemed to split her mind further with each passing hour.

I made a dinner that April refused to eat and I could barely touch myself. I kept looking in on her, wondering if her depression had at last overwhelmed everything and turned her catatonic, but she was lucid when I asked her questions. Nor did she brush me away when I sat on the edge of the bed and gently stroked her forehead.

At eleven I finally convinced her to have a shower, and could hardly suppress my relief when she emerged clean and smiling, almost sane, almost back to me.

To get April to bed I made a sexy joke of it, teasing her, using her own body's response against her. She let me coax her onto the mattress but even my most tender attempts at foreplay failed. I didn't mind. With all my anxiety, I was probably even less in the mood than her. That she was in my arms was enough.

It had been a long day, full of worry and work, and I was exhausted. Confident she was warm and safe, I drifted off.

Only to wake cold and dread-filled.

The bed was empty. Outside, Holly was going crazy. Panic had me shooting upright. I looked toward the door, hoping to see a glow from the bathroom light, that she'd simply needed the loo in the night and would be back any moment.

Then beyond Holly's barks I heard the noise. The rev of a car, the whoops.

I jumped out of bed so fast I fell, banging my head on the side table. Ignoring the hot trickle across my scalp, I pulled on jeans and a jumper and sprinted down the hall, wasting more precious seconds pulling on boots.

I yanked the door open, the car noise and

yahoos were still going but so was another sound. A wailing so animalistic it didn't seem human.

April.

As I sprinted the car's engine changed. I reached the paddock just as it was broad-siding down the hill toward the hole they'd cut in the fence. The plastic used to replace the car's smashed back windscreen flapped where the tape holding it in place had come unstuck. For a heartbeat I thought of running after them, but April's heart-wrenching screams were shattering my soul.

Laughter carried as I vaulted and ran for her. Then the car shot through the opening, bounced over the drain, skidded onto the road, and was gone.

The void of quiet it left behind was terrifying.

April was in her nightie in the centre of LOVE. Except it didn't spell love any more. What was once a painstakingly arranged garden of flowers was now a mess of mud and tyre tracks. As I approached, she began to crawl on her hands and knees, keening horribly, picking at destroyed flowers and trying to dig them back into the soil.

I knelt beside her and held her to me. 'I'm sorry, I'm sorry, I'm sorry.'

No matter how tightly I held her, how soothing I tried to be, she wouldn't stop making that noise or struggling against me. LOVE was ruined. There would be no birthday present for Daniel. No celebration of a mother's love for her lost little boy.

No peace.

Her agony brought me to tears.

She pushed me away and scampered for more plants. The moon was half full and the light poor but April was mad with determination. Muttering to herself between keens, she searched for plants, dug holes with her bare hands and patted them into place. There was no way of telling if she was even planting them in the right spot. It was too dark and the letters too obscured by the car's tracks.

She began to shiver, from cold, from shock, her teeth knocking and her breath shuddery. I was helpless in my attempts to get her back to the house. She bit and scratched and punched me. When I locked my arms around her she screamed and kicked and flung herself around so hard I was scared I'd hurt her and let her go. Immediately she dropped back to her knees and resumed her intense planting.

I stood in hopeless despair, my heart breaking for her, aware I had to do something.

An ambulance seemed the obvious choice. April was sick, really sick. There was no hiding it any more. Yet I was still stupid enough to think that I could handle it, that I could save her the trauma of being removed from Rainbow on the day she'd been waiting so excitedly for. That she wouldn't be forced to spend the day her little boy should have turned ten in some anonymous cold hospital.

I'd promised to never abandon her. I couldn't betray that.

I crouched down next to her and stroked her

hair. 'April, I'm going to go to the cottage for a minute and grab you some warm clothes, okay?'

She didn't respond. Another plant, all its leaves broken and flowers missing, went into the ground with a satisfied mutter.

'I won't be long.'

I hesitated, taking a last look at her, and ran.

After a brief fight, she let me thread one of my jumpers over her head and cloak her with a wool-lined oilskin coat. Getting jeans on her was out of the question, but while she was on her knees I slipped long socks on her legs and her banana-coloured rubber boots on her feet. Finally, I pulled a woollen football beanie over her head and let her go again, resting on my haunches with a tear sliding down my cheek in fear for my poor broken April.

In the pocket of my jeans was Sebastian's card.

'April, I'm sorry.'

If she heard she didn't acknowledge it. With the card in my hand, I pulled out my phone and made the call that I hoped would save her life.

TWENTY-FOUR

Some time before dawn the fight seemed to leave April. She slumped on her knees, breathing heavily, and stared at the mess around her. In her haste to recover LOVE she'd trampled more plants than she'd saved, and the site was more mangled than ever.

Sensing she was ready to leave it, I fetched the blanket I'd tried unsuccessfully to wrap around her during the night and laid it over her shoulders.

'Come on,' I said, lifting her gently and kissing her forehead.

She walked like an old woman, bowed and arthritic, her feet dragging and slipping in her rubber boots. In the house I sat her in front of the fire and poured tea from the thermos I'd prepared earlier, but had no success in getting her to accept.

Although it broke me up inside, I'd left April alone several times to tend the fire, check my phone for instructions from Sebastian, and refill the thermos. Keeping her warm had become my main priority. The rest would take the care of experts.

I wrapped her hands around the mug. For a brief second, I thought I saw her mind reach for me. I cupped her face and studied her.

'You're safe, April,' but the imploring

expression, if it ever existed, was gone. Longing and love can play tricks on us all.

I set about tidying her up as best I could. She was caked in mud. It was in her hair, on her clothes, threaded down the inside of her boots. Even the corners of her eyes were thick with it.

I talked to her as I worked. Nonsense words, the way you'd talk to a child, feigning amazement at all the places she'd managed to get dirt. How I'd have her cleaned up and in bed in no time. To my relief she stayed compliant, and I prayed it was because she lacked the energy to fight and not that her spirit was broken. I sponged her down as best I could, rinsed her hair and dried it with her hairdryer. Not once did she speak.

Dawn began to creep into the room. With each layering of light I felt my anxiety worsen. Sebastian and the doctor he was bringing wouldn't be far away, and with them a future I could only guess at. Even then I hung onto the hope that a few drugs might fix her, that they'd put her to bed and leave her in my care. But deep in my heart I knew that was impossible.

When she was as clean as I could make her, I tried to lead her to bed but I should have known better. As we passed Daniel's room she wavered and reached out. Tears covered her cheeks. Her mouth trembled.

I let her go. Today was his birthday. Without LOVE this was her only way of being with him.

She crossed to his astronaut bed and lay down. I followed and, with a little encouragement, managed to get her under the quilt and tuck it around her. She curled up in the foetal position and closed her eyes.

I stayed, hand on her hair, stroking her forehead with my thumb, until her breathing became regular and I was sure she was asleep. Then I kissed her softly and whispered the words I should have shouted from the start.

At the door I turned to watch her a little longer. The pain of loss I felt had to be nothing compared to hers, and yet still it tore at me. This was my doing. She'd needed help and I'd done nothing until it was too late. And now I was going to lose her completely.

April had known the truth of it all along. Love hurts.

I pressed my head against the door frame and banged it a couple of times, wishing I could keep banging harder and harder until I knocked myself out.

The ongoing wait for Sebastian to travel from Melbourne was the most miserable hour and half of my life. But the minutes that followed his and then the doctor's arrival were infinitely worse.

The Aston Martin was first, sliding to a halt near the verandah. Sebastian's feet were like thunder on the floorboards. I leapt up to stop him before he made even more racket.

'Where is she?'

I pressed my finger to my lips and led him away from the house, toward April's paddock. 'Sleeping.'

'Is she all right?'

I hesitated before answering, feeling like I was

passing sentence. 'No. She's . . .' I shook my head, not knowing how to describe her. I took him closer to the fence instead. 'She was out here all night, trying to put LOVE back together.'

Sebastian squinted at the paddock. 'What the hell was she trying to do?'

'Talk to Daniel.'

He rubbed his forehead. 'I should never have let her buy this place.'

The way things had turned out I couldn't disagree, but there were times when April was happy at Rainbow, when she laughed properly and smiled and found wonder in things.

A large van with blacked out windows turned off the road. Sebastian and I headed over to meet it. The driver backed into the drive and stopped a few metres from Sebastian's Aston Martin.

'You might want to move that,' the driver advised when he climbed out.

One look and the man annoyed me. I'm a fairly solid bloke but he was bigger. It wasn't that which I minded, but the swagger in the way he walked, the way he spoke as if just being alive put him in charge.

A slope-shouldered, balding man also alighted. He paused and looked me up and down before addressing Sebastian, but it was me who answered.

'She's inside, asleep on her son's bed.' I stepped in front of him and from the corner of my eye saw boofhead brace himself for action. 'She's been up all night.'

'Okay. Let's take a look at her.'

I thought of how she'd briefly spoken to me with her eyes, when I'd handed her the cup. The moment of lucidity I wasn't sure had been real. There was gratitude in that brief connection and a plea. The more I saw of these people the more I wished I'd believed that silent appeal.

'Don't wake her.'

He sighed and went to push past me.

'Tristan,' said Sebastian as I went to step in front again. 'He's a doctor. He knows what he's doing. She needs help. Let him and the nurse provide it.'

Reluctantly, I stepped back, my guts churning.

Throwing me a last warning look to stay put, Sebastian followed them inside.

Minutes passed. I paced in the early morning cold, Holly on my heels. The dog had been with us all night. She had to be as exhausted as I was but she stayed with me, ignoring my order to go to the shed. I didn't have the heart to tell her again.

I spun around as the screen door opened. Sebastian came out and held it wide. The doctor stepped onto the verandah. April stood in the doorway, peering outside in confusion. Her eyes settled on me and a faint smile tilted her mouth. I smiled back, feeling sick.

Boofhead tried to guide her onward.

April frowned. She looked at Sebastian, her voice hesitant. 'What are you doing?'

'You need to come home.'

'No.' She shook her head and tried to step back. 'No.'

Boofhead blocked her way with his body. April

turned and lunged at him. Fingers out, attempting to scratch with nails she didn't realise had broken off in the night. An awful, unearthly screech shattered the day.

'April!' I bolted for her but Sebastian reached me first. He shoved me as I tried to climb up the verandah. Unbalanced, I fell back but quickly regained my feet. My hands curled into fists, ready to fight.

'For Christ's sake, Tristan, you're not helping!'

'He's hurting her!'

'He's not.' Keeping one hand flat in the centre of my chest, Sebastian jerked a look over his shoulder. 'You can see that for yourself.'

I knew Sebastian was right. Boofhead hadn't laid a finger on April. He merely kept his arms raised to ward off her blows and his body stiff, a wall preventing her escape. The doctor had disappeared into the back of the van.

Giving up, she whirled around. 'Tristan, help me!'

The words dragged at me. The woman I loved was asking for my help. I couldn't refuse.

Sebastian pressed his hand harder into my chest. 'Don't.'

Boofhead met my gaze over April's head, his eyes absent of the challenge I'd expected. What I saw was sympathy. My shoulders dropped. I breathed out hard.

April's eyes widened, a sob escaped. 'Tristan?'

I shook my head.

'Tristan, you promised!'

She was pleading with me, calling on my oath

not to abandon her, and still I remained where I was. The moment when she recognised my betrayal will remain with me forever. Her head flopped and for a few seconds she stood limp, all faith destroyed.

And then she became fury unleashed. April threw herself forward, catching Boofhead off guard. Sebastian went to grab her only for April to respond with flying fists, kicks and snapping teeth. I tried to help but she was a whirl of uncontrolled mayhem, the same as she'd been when I tried to drag her from the paddock.

Boofhead recovered and, using his thick arms, locked her down. The doctor emerged from the van and exchanged a look with Boofhead, who nodded. As the needle went in, April kept her accusing gaze on me, forcing me to witness the shutting down of all that made her precious. Making me face what I had done.

I had betrayed the woman who'd made me into the man I wanted to be. Whose tears I had kissed when she cried, whose body I had held in passion, who I'd given my heart and my honour. The woman I was meant to love.

I was no hero Tristan.

I was Judas.

TWENTY-FIVE

It had been five weeks and three days since April was taken away. I couldn't scrub the betrayal from my skin. It was like a permanent layer of rank sweat that only I could smell.

But I had to do it.

Every day I rang Sebastian to find out how she was faring at the clinic, when I could see her. Rainbow wasn't right without April. I wasn't right. The world wasn't. Nothing was.

One morning he swore and lost his temper at me. 'Jesus Christ, Tristan, can't you work it out? She doesn't want to see you!'

I had no idea I could hurt more than I already did until I heard those words.

There was no response for that. Hanging up, I stood with Holly in April's paddock, staring at the slope below the cairn where she used to sit, wondering what the hell I was going to do with my life.

Go on, I supposed. It's what you did. And I had so much: family, friends, good health, a dog who seemed to like me.

But I didn't have April.

I sank to the ground, pulled my legs up and rested my wrists on my knees, staring at nothing, while in my mind I saw April dancing, black hair flowing, green eyes on fire, her laughter like magic in the air.

And I saw at last what it was like for her. I saw her the way she must have seen Daniel.

I lowered my head.

Oh, God, I was lost.

TWENTY-SIX

Shearing arrived with the close of spring. As a favour to Dad a couple of blokes from the team who'd done Oakvale came over to Rainbow to sort mine. They were done before lunch. With everything that had happened I hadn't the guts to buy more stock, despite the land crying out for it. I hadn't the will for it either. Sadness had made me too weary.

Because some of April's ewes still had traces of colour in their wool and we were worried about contamination, Dad, my brothers and I used the rest of the day to sort them ourselves. None of us are shearers but we managed okay, even if there were quite a few second cuts, and Patrick managed to stick his clippers right through the hamstring of one of the rattier ones. The wool wasn't going for sale anyway. I was going to store it for April. In case.

I'd been doing a lot of that. I'd go to toss some piece of scrap aside and stop, thinking that April might want it for her art. I'd take photos with my phone – of the sheep, Holly, the landscape, nature – in case April changed her mind and wanted to know what was happening at Rainbow.

I put on a barbecue after shearing. Andrea brought Gran, and Wendell came with my niece and nephew. Jeremy's new girlfriend arrived too and so Rainbow played host to my whole family. The kids ran around, squealing as they chased the dogs and each other. The smell of frying onions and sausages drifted. Mum had made pavlova with fresh passionfruit pulp on top because she knew it was my favourite. Dad and the boys stood around with beers, watching the barbecue and talking sport and livestock sales.

As the sun was beginning to drop, I ducked into the house for another beer. I'd been okay, a bit quiet, and watching Jeremy with Stacey was hard, but when I went to push open the door on my way out, I stopped. The happy family scene walloped me in the chest so hard I couldn't breathe. I backed inside, dumped my beer on the bench and strode for my bedroom, desperate to make it before my throat closed over with grief and heartbreak, and I cracked in front of everyone.

Her scarf was on top of my chest of drawers. I sat on the bed with it on my lap and my hand on top and stared at the wall, thinking about her. What was she doing? Was she still at the clinic or home? It'd be Christmas soon. Surely they'd let her home for that.

My head flopped. I didn't even know where home for April was. I hardly knew anything.

Except that I loved her and always would.

A knock sounded at the door frame. Mum came in and sat alongside me. She looked at the scarf. 'April's?'

Unable to speak, I nodded.

A couple of weeks after she'd been taken away,

Sebastian sent a truck and workers for her things and the Range Rover. I'd walked around the house afterward, looking for a trace of her, but there was nothing. The scarf I found when I went to clean up the shed. It was buried in the nest of straw we'd made, and when I lifted it to my nose I caught a trace of her. Until then, although I'd come close, I hadn't let myself cry over April or what I'd done, but in that moment I lost it completely. Now the scarf had my tears mixed with April's spirit. All I had left.

Mum took my hand and held it. While no one really knew what happened that night they were all aware that it was something bad. April was gone. And no matter how much I tried to hide it, everyone could see my heartbreak.

Andrea and Mum fretted and fussed. Dad kept offering to come over and help or ringing to ask if I'd mind giving him a hand at home, even though he had three other sons to take the load. They were concerned and wanted to keep an eye on me, so for their sake I played along. I'd made enough of a mess without upsetting my family as well.

'Have you heard anything?'

I shook my head.

'You could write, perhaps.'

'I don't have an address.' I didn't have anything except her scarf.

'What about Junior?'

I looked at Mum. Then leaned across and kissed her cheek. 'Thanks.'

She squeezed my hand tighter and I saw her

eyes filling. 'You know we all love you, don't you?'

I nodded. I did. My family radiated love. I wish April could have felt it too.

'I'm okay, Mum.'

She squeezed my hand tightly. 'We've all been a bit worried.'

'I know.' I kissed her cheek again and rose to take April's scarf to its place on the chest of drawers, where I laid it, carefully folded. For a moment I kept my palm on the soft wool before turning away and draping my arm around Mum's shoulders.

Thanks to her I had hope.

I had Junior.

TWENTY-SEVEN

'Tristan, how are you, mate?'

I hovered in the doorway of Junior's office with my precious envelope.

He waved at me. 'Come in. Take a seat.'

I looked at the envelope, still unsure if I was doing the right thing, but what other option did I have? Sebastian wasn't answering my calls or texts. Every call to April's phone went to voice mail, every text was left unanswered. Junior and my envelope were all I had left.

It wasn't a letter. What was in my head seemed impossible to put down into words. Instead, I'd printed out one of the photographs I'd taken of Rainbow and written a single word on the back of it.

Sometimes, when I laid in bed, I'd think of the things April had done for Daniel and wondered if I could perhaps talk to April the same way. If I could find a paddock of my own, one that the sun danced over, and carve my feelings into it. Or plant sunflowers into words. Paint SORRY onto the grass with fluorescent paint so that it glowed night and day.

Except sorry wouldn't bring her back. It wasn't powerful enough. Nothing was.

My betrayal was wretched, but I had done the

right thing. Nothing was more important than April's life. Not my love, not hers. If forsaking us meant saving her then there was no choice. Only action.

Ignoring his invitation to sit, I held out the envelope to Junior. 'Can you see that April Tremayne gets this?'

He took it and laid it on his desk, regarding it for a moment. Then he looked up and held my gaze. 'I guess it had to happen.'

I had no idea what he was on about.

He tapped the envelope. 'Your resignation.'

I wasn't up to explaining. Making up that envelope, coming into his office, had been difficult enough. 'You can get it to her?'

He nodded.

I breathed out hard. I hadn't been sure if Junior still knew how to get in touch, or if he even worked for her any more.

'Are you sure about this?'

I shook my head. I wasn't sure about anything but I had to try.

I left Junior to his confusion and went home to Rainbow. It would take a few days at least for the photograph to get to her. Even if it made it that far, there was a good chance she might tear it up unopened. Maybe Sebastian was vetting all her mail, or the clinic.

God, please let her not still be at the clinic. Let her be better.

Let her dance once more with joy.

I carried on at the farm as usual. There were times when I managed to go a few hours without thinking about April, or about the photo I'd sent or the word I'd written on the back. Sometimes I'd have to stop what I was doing and catch my breath, reclaiming it from the fear that had stolen it away.

The photo was right but the word . . .

Longing kept me wandering April's paddock. Usually I walked it in the late evening, when the shadows were stringy and the colours pretty. The resilience of nature never ceases to comfort me. Despite the destruction it had endured, LOVE refused to go away. Although the word itself was mainly obliterated, a few plants struggled on, popping up flowers and glossy leaves amongst the white clover and ryegrass. In the right light, the view from the slope below the cairn still showed LOVE's faint outline. I took photos in case April would want to know.

A week passed. Then another.

The week before Christmas I finally admitted to myself that the photo hadn't worked. That there really was no hope she'd come back, that I'd ever see her again.

I felt hollow and sunken. Every step seemed to take effort. Noticing a change, Mum and Andrea took to calling around again and dragging me out to events that I didn't want to attend. For their sake, I forced myself to act normal, retreating back into myself the moment I returned to Rainbow.

It was lunchtime the day before Christmas eve, and I'd just pulled the ute away from the cottage, Holly in the back, the passenger seat loaded with presents, when I caught the glint of sunlight on metal. My heart sank. I wasn't in the mood for a visitor. Wrapping the presents had left me miserable. I'd been thinking about April again, imagining a future that we'd never live. The house full of laughter as our children raced to see what Santa had brought. Our first Christmas hosting my family. April and me stringing the house with fake mistletoe so we could kiss in every doorway.

I thought about hiding, but good manners prevented my escape. I pressed down on the accelerator, expecting to meet my visitor halfway between the cottage and April's house but no car appeared.

My stomach tensed further with each roll of the ute's tyres.

Sunshine on metal gave way to form. I braked hard, the gravel skid as loud as my thumping heart.

Sebastian's Aston Martin was in April's yard.

I pressed my head against the wheel, my hands fisted and sweating.

It was nearly Christmas. Sebastian couldn't do this. I had to have a little longer. A little more of Rainbow. A little more of April.

In the New Year. They could sell it then. A new year, a new start. I might have the strength then.

It took a lot of effort to make myself drive on.

Holly licked my hand as I stepped out. I petted her, taking comfort from the dog, using her affection to anchor me when everything was spinning.

A few minutes passed. Minutes when each

breath only made the fear in my chest sharpen and stab harder.

Finally, the screen door pushed open. And my heart stuttered and then began to boom like the deepest of drums.

April stepped out onto the verandah. Her dark hair was loose and even longer than I remembered. The breeze blew tresses around her face, obscuring her expression. She wore faded jeans and a green singlet that hugged her slim body and showed off tanned skin.

She was the most beautiful, perfect thing I'd ever seen.

I wanted to run to her but my legs were like stilts.

She began to walk toward me. No smile. Just an intense green stare.

Behind her, the door swung open again and Sebastian moved outside to lean against a wall with his arms crossed.

April paused a careful distance in front of me. Too far to touch, but still here, like a dream. Perhaps that's what she was. A dream, like Daniel had been to her.

I couldn't breathe. I couldn't talk.

She blinked, dislodging a tear.

And I broke with it. 'I'm sorry. I shouldn't have . . .' I dropped my hands. No matter what the cost, what I did was right. 'I had no choice. I loved you. I wanted to marry you. Wanted us to grow old together here, at Rainbow.'

'And now?'

'Now I just want see you happy, even if it's

without me.'

Another tear fell. She looked away. 'I'm trying to be.'

I sensed a 'but' hovering and waited. April sucked on her bottom lip and swiped at her tears with the heels of her hands. The wind rose, whistling a momentary lament, and faded.

I went to step closer and hesitated. She was no longer mine to touch. I could see that now. This was goodbye at last. She'd allowed me the peace to know she was okay and now it was time to move on.

'I hope you find it, April. I really do.'

She opened her mouth then shoved her knuckles in it and shook her head.

I gestured toward the ute, forcing my voice normal. 'I'd better get going. Leave you to it. Christmas presents to deliver.' Before I could change my mind, I leaned forward and kissed April's forehead, my eyes closing at the contact. 'Thank you.'

Those steps to the ute were the longest I'd ever taken. Holly whined and I scrubbed her head, then I held my hand up to Sebastian in farewell.

April stepped forward. 'For what?'

I opened the ute door. Time to go. Time to get out of here before I crumbled completely.

She ran to me and yanked my arm from the door. 'For what, Tristan?'

'For giving me the best year of my life.' I smiled and touched her wet cheek, my own eyes stinging. 'Take care, April.'

Through the rear vision mirror I watched her

return to Sebastian. I saw her collapse in his arms. I saw her fists pound his chest and her shoulders heave with sobs. I felt my own grief rise like a clawing living thing in my chest and scrape my insides as it tried to escape.

But still I kept driving.

TWENTY-EIGHT

The New Year kicked on. I applied for a couple of jobs, one across the border in South Australia, the other near Branxholme, to the south east. I was asked to interview for both and withdrew from both. I couldn't handle the thought of leaving Rainbow. It was too much like leaving her.

Though I was trying to move on, I couldn't stop thinking back to the day she'd returned to say goodbye. The way she'd looked at me. The unsaid 'but' I'd heard at the end of her claim that she was trying to be happy.

At the time I'd interpreted it as meaning she could never be happy, that without Daniel the world would be forever dark, because that was how I felt without her in my life. I understood. There was a scar on our souls that would never fade.

But one thing I had a lot of was thinking time, and I'd rolled that moment over and over in my head a thousand times. Now I wondered if perhaps she hadn't meant something else. If perhaps the trip to Rainbow held another purpose. One left unfulfilled because I'd chosen to drive away.

I began to fill in the 'buts' myself.

I'm trying to be happy but I can't without

Rainbow.

I'm trying to be happy but I can't without you.

Daydreams can be cruel things.

Valentine's Day came without me realising. I'd been to the bank and was walking back to the car when I noticed the newsagent's window. The display shone bright with fluffy toys, sentimental cards, fake roses and red streamers. Easy to dismiss as meaningless commerciality.

Until I saw the foil balloons.

My jaw clenched. I wheeled away as fast as I could without running, and drove rapidly back to Rainbow, banging the heel of my hand against the wheel in frustration. Cursing the hurt I couldn't recover from. Damning the love I couldn't stop.

Wishing she'd come back to me.

I drank too many beers that night, passing the painful hours on the front porch with Holly by my side and April's scarf on my lap. At some point in the darkness, I sent April an 'Are you happy?' text message, only to throw my phone hard into the bushes when I received no reply.

Two weeks later a thick envelope appeared in the roadside mail drop. The embossed return address said it was from an art gallery in the posh Melbourne suburb of South Yarra. I stood beside the old drum that made up Rainbow's mailbox and stared at the envelope while the ute's engine chugged and Holly whined at me from the back tray.

April. It had to be.

I balanced it on my lap all the way to the cottage, one hand on the expensive paper as if I could feel her through it. The only pulse though, was mine. A fast beat of hope and anxiety. I sat at the kitchen table and used a knife to slit the envelope. A glossy card lay inside. I pulled it free.

Something else slid out with it.

The photo I'd sent April.

An image of a rainbow that had formed one magical afternoon over her house and paddock, the flowers from her installation speckled amongst the green as though the rainbow had shed pieces of itself, like confetti. A vision so special, so perfect, that I'd had to take multiple shots to get it right because my hands kept trembling and my chest kept crushing in on itself with hurt and longing

The photo on the back of which I'd written, in simple capitals, LOVE.

My last chance. Sent back.

I closed my eyes as anguish tore at me and forced myself to breathe it away. There was still the card. I picked it up and read.

It was an invitation to an exhibition in a month's time. April's exhibition. With my name picked out in gold calligraphy. She wanted me to come.

I rubbed my face and picked up the photo again and turned it over. Below my carefully spelled out LOVE April had written her name.

LOVE

April

Perhaps a plea. Perhaps a signature.

Either way I was going to find out.

TWENTY-NINE

A year ago there wasn't a chance in hell I'd ever go to a place like this on my own. A year ago I would have stood in the corner with baboon's bum in full flourish, making an idiot of myself simply by being there.

But I wasn't the same man as a year ago.

The bloke on the door looked at me suspiciously when I handed over my invitation, and then started when he consulted his list.

'Mr Blake, April will be delighted to hear you made it.'

I nodded, barely looking at him, my focus on inside where people milled and wait staff circled the room with drinks and food. With each flash of dark hair my stomach hopped then slid down again as a turn of profile revealed it wasn't April.

'Is she here?'

'Inside.' He looked past me to the next person in line. I took the hint and moved on.

The invitation hadn't mentioned a dress code so I'd decided on my good moleskins and a well-ironed blue shirt. Clothes that made me look exactly what I was – a farmer up from the country – but made me feel safe. At least April wouldn't be able to miss me among the endless black.

A few heads turned my way when I walked up

the stairs and paused, searching for April, and instead spotted Sebastian standing with a skinny blonde. I nodded, and as I went to walk toward him, I caught a flash of long black hair out of the corner of my eye.

My heart clenched to the point of pain.

April was talking to two men and a woman, her hands forming pictures in the air as she explained something. Her eyes were wide with excitement, her audience rapt, nodding and smiling. Suddenly her hands stopped fluttering. She stilled, head tilted as though listening. Slowly she began to turn.

Our gazes met. For several heartbeats we were alone, caught in our silent communion, then someone pushed into me and by the time I'd shifted and muttered excuse me, April had turned away.

A waiter passed with a tray of drinks. Needing a moment to calm down, I grabbed one and walked to the side of the room, but my elation kept bubbling through.

I'd seen April.

And she was happy.

A few people had broken away from the main group, like me, and were touring the gallery, stopping at pedestals upon which metal sculptures sat. They were small pieces, each about thirty centimetres square and each with an overriding, multi-layered arch made from coloured glass.

Rainbows over landscapes.

Rainbows over Rainbow.

I checked the crowd without success and

returned to the sculptures, analysing her art, what she meant by it. What it meant that she wanted me to see it.

There were rainbows over hills, over creeks, over paddocks full of sheep. Rainbows over isolated cottages. Rainbows over flowers and trees. Some of the rainbows were tiny, like a fragile blessing over a select piece of the earth. Others ran from one side of the landscape to the other, cascading colour over the metal ground beneath.

At the back of the room, balanced a large white plinth and lit from above by a chandelier of stage lights, was a feature sculpture. I walked toward it, wondering if this would be my message.

From a central valley, ripples of metal rose to form hill crests. Above and across the landscape's diagonal length ran a metal and glass rainbow. Underneath, in the heart of the valley, a small boy walked with his back to the viewer, determinedly making his way to the rainbow's end. Standing alone at the peak of the tallest hill was a woman in a long skirt, one hand raised in farewell.

My throat turned thick with sorrow. For April. For the son she'd had to bury.

Someone came to stand beside me. I didn't need to look to know who it was.

'They're beautiful,' I said.

'Thank you.' Her fingers brushed mine. For a brief second they hooked and let go. A shy touch, as if she wasn't sure it was welcome.

'April?'

She lifted her head.

'I love you.'

Her eyes turned huge. Her mouth parted as though to say something and then a woman swept from the crowd, exclaiming about people April *must* meet, and dragged her off, leaving me alone.

I walked out of the gallery. It was a solid four hour drive back to Rainbow and the crowd showed no sign of dispersing. April would be busy for a long time yet. It was her night, her triumph. She didn't need me disrupting it any further. Besides, whatever else we had to say to one another could wait. What was more time after what had already passed?

Against the thrum of the road and the swallow of darkness, my mind sieved through the evening. The way she'd regarded me on arrival. How she'd looked over her shoulder at me as she was dragged away. The breathtakingly sad beauty of her work.

Forty-five kilometres from home my phone lit up. I glanced at the screen and immediately pulled over onto the grassy verge.

'April.' I smiled at the sound her name made in the darkness.

'Where are you?'

'Nearly home.'

She didn't say anything for a long while. 'Why?'

'Because Rainbow is where I'm with you.' I let her think on that. 'You looked happy tonight. I'm glad.'

Her soft goodbye left me staring at the night, praying.

THIRTY

Autumn was refusing to break. The hills remained bleached-blonde from the dry summer but I wasn't worried. Rainbow's low stocking rate meant we still had plenty of feed.

April's Suffolks were sway-bellied with lambs that would shortly drop. My own the same. Although Dad had advised against it, I'd decided to buy some cattle for Rainbow. He was worried, as Mum was, that my position was too tenuous to risk it. But Dad didn't know what I did. He didn't feel the change in the air. He didn't hear the wind whispering encouragement as it curled around the hills and brushed my shirt like a caress.

He hadn't seen the way April had looked when I told her I loved her.

He didn't understand how dumb with hope I was.

That morning, Dad and I had travelled across the border to a Hereford stud where only his caution prevented me from buying on the spot. I knew I'd be back though, and my mood was high as I turned into Rainbow. Lambing would start soon and it was hard not to feel excited about my first drop. I wondered, as I always did, what April would make of it. Whether it would make her sad because of her own loss, or if she'd delight in this show of life.

There was a pine box sitting on the door mat when I pulled up at the cottage. Holly barked at me, tail wagging as though she couldn't wait for my arrival home so I could open the present for her.

The box was unlabelled, the contents heavy. Cautious, I took it inside and laid it on the table and stared at it for a while.

Then my heart began to thud.

I ran for the garden shed and the basic tools I kept there, returning with a flatheaded screwdriver. I used the screwdriver to dig under the lid, prising it up, one board at a time, exposing a mass of raffia type stuffing. I cleared a little away.

And caught the gleam of coloured glass.

Breath racing, I dug deeper.

Cold metal touched my fingers.

A strange moan came out of my mouth. Hope, longing, fear.

Terrified of breaking it, I tried to take my time. It was hard though, so hard. She'd been here. She'd left this precious thing for me. I had to know where she saw our future.

The world condensed to a box. Movements clumsy, I dragged the hanks of raffia out and cast them to the floor. The lid slipped off the table, taking the screwdriver with it. The noise made me jolt but I kept clearing until my hands could slide freely under the sculpture's base. I lifted it out and set it on the table and blew the last of the packing away.

I stared, my throat thick, my heart bloated.

A rainbow shone over a house at the top of a hill. Across from it was another hill, topped with a cairn. Below the house were two figures. A man stood near the top of the slope looking down at a woman with her arms outstretched and her head thrown back, her face covered in rainbow light. The twirl sent her hair and skirt spinning out, their waves shot with more colour.

April dancing at Rainbow.

For me.

I stroked the sculpture once, then turned and sprinted outside.

THIRTY-ONE

She was waiting on the verandah of the house.

I slowed to a jog and stopped at the gate. The sprint had left me panting but it was the sight of her that sucked the last of my breath.

Joy. Fear. Longing.

Hope. Growing stronger with every inhalation.

Not for a second did I let my gaze leave hers. I walked the drive with our eyes locked, so full of love and excitement that my fluttery heart threatened to launch me skyward.

I halted in front of her and simply stared, taking her in like the miracle she was.

She smiled a little and I knew we would be all right.

'Welcome home, Ms Tremayne.'

'It's good to be home, Mr Blake.'

I stroked her soft hair as I studied her face. 'Are you happy?'

She slid her arms around me. 'I am now.'

I bent my head and kissed her.

The best kiss of my life.

EPILOGUE

I didn't realise happiness could be like this. Or love.

But April taught me that it could be big and bright and rainbow-coloured and last forever.

She has a proper studio here at Rainbow now where she creates beautiful metal sculptures of animals and plants and children. Of life. Her rainbow period has passed. The grief attached to those creations somehow softened by their message. It will never fade fully. I hate the burden she must carry and do my utmost to ease it, but I know it will always remain.

Because I understand now that love hurts. That is its cost.

Which is why when I find April alone in her paddock it's hard to control my panic. Those days and nights from long ago are my scars as much as hers, and though the years are passing fast, their impact remains.

In the first few months after her return I could barely leave her alone for fear. She did her best to reassure me that her mind had mended, but I couldn't shake the memories. April in the rain as she watched the collapse of JOY. Her obsession. The belief she communed with Daniel. The helplessness of watching her shivering and scrounging in the dark as she frantically tried to put LOVE back together.

And I still had to recover from the knowledge that, justified or not, I'd betrayed her, the woman I loved. That I'd broken my promise and with it her trust.

There were days back then when I'd worry myself sick that she'd never be able to believe in me again. I'd get silent and clingy, embarrassing myself. But I couldn't stop. When I finally admitted my fear she smiled and shook her head, and told me that because of what I did she trusted me more. It took me a long time to figure that one out but in the end I got it.

Whatever it took, whatever the cost, I would sacrifice my own heart for her.

The moment I understood I sought her out, got down on one knee and asked her to marry me. April had laughed and with tears glistening her eyes asked what took me so long.

'I'm not much of a talker,' I replied.

That only made her laugh even more delightedly. Then she'd flung her arms around me and kissed me so hard I fell backwards. We rolled like a couple of dumb teenagers in the middle of the yard, which then led to other things that were annoyingly interrupted by the arrival of Mum and Andrea.

We made up for it though.

There are children at Rainbow now. Beautiful healthy children who fill the air with joy. Our youngest Mitchell is nearly three and looks like me. His manner though, is all his mother's. April says he's going to be a heartbreaker when he's older. He has the charm, that's for sure. Isla is five now and as shy as I used to be, hiding behind her mother's legs when faced with strangers, not talking much. April blames herself for Isla's shyness. Daniel's death meant she suffered terrible fears in the children's early years, and even now she can still be a bit overprotective. But I think Isla just takes after me. I hope one day she'll find someone who makes her into the woman she's meant to be, as April made me into the man I wanted to be.

I can see her from the house. She's sitting at the top of her paddock with her arms wrapped around her knees, staring toward the horizon. My stomach flips with worry. I can't help it. I can't help my length of stride as I go to her, and I'm grateful the kids are today at Oakvale, stolen again, as they so often are, by their doting grandmother.

I settle alongside April and take her hand.

I'm still not much of a talker but a lot of that is simply because there are times when April and I don't need to talk. We communicate with looks or touches. The silent language of people who love one another. Taking her hand means I'm there, that she'll always be okay because I'll make sure she is.

She glances at me and back to the horizon. 'There are some days when I can't believe my life.'

I lift her hand and kiss the back of it. There are days when I, too, wonder how it all happened. Something this monumental has to be fate, the answer to some problem the universe had to solve using us.

'I think Daniel really did bring me here. I followed his trail as he scattered himself across the sky until he brought me to Rainbow. He gave me you and Isla and Mitchell, and now he's giving me even more.' She holds my gaze and sees my worry. A smile turns her face radiant. 'I'm pregnant again.'

I burst with pride and pure, white-hot love.

'Happy?'

In answer I kiss her stupid and then kiss her some more until she's laughing and pushing me away. I cradle April against me as we take in the vivid blue horizon and say our silent thanks.

Definitely happy.

Dear Reader,

Thank you so much for buying and reading *April's Rainbow*. For me this book is what romance authors sometimes refer to as a book of the heart. I hope it has moved you as much as it did me.

Would you like to know when my next release comes available plus gain access to exclusive content, news and giveaways? Please sign up to my newsletter by visiting:

www.cathrynhein.com/newsletter

If you'd like to find out more about me and my books, including the inspiration behind *April's Rainbow*, you'll find it all at cathrynhein.com. Join me on Facebook and Twitter using @CathrynHein. I love to connect!

Help others find their next read by leaving a review of *April's Rainbow* on your favourite book website.

Now please enjoy this excerpt from my sweet rural novella Summer and the Groomsman.

Warm wishes,

Cathryn

Summer
AND THE GROOMSMAN
CATHRYN
HEIN
A Levenham Love Story

Summer
AND THE GROOMSMAN
CATHRYN HEIN

It's Levenham's wedding of the year but unlucky-in-love Harry Argyle has more on his mind than being groomsman.

After yet again nearly colliding with an escaped horse while driving home to the family farm, Harry Argyle comes face-to-face with its pretty owner, and doesn't hold back his disapproval.

Confronted by a bad-tempered giant on a dark country road, beautician and new arrival in town Summer Taylor doesn't know who to be more afraid for: herself or her darling horse Binky. It's not her fault Binky keeps escaping. The alcoholic owner of the paddock she rents won't fix the fence and Binky can be sneaky when it comes to filling his stomach. But no matter how big and muscled the bully, she refuses to be intimidated.

When Harry's wedding party book a session at the day spa where Summer works, both she and Harry are horrified to be paired together. Grudgingly, they agree to make the most of it - only for the session to spiral into disaster. Realising he's made a dill of himself in front of sweet Summer yet again, Harry vows to set things right.

Summer isn't about to easily forgive the man who called her horse stupid, no matter how brave and kind, but with everyone on Harry's side, even fate, resistance is hard. Can these two find love or will Summer's wayward horse put his hoof in it again?

A sweet rural romance novella from Cathryn Hein, best-selling author of *The Falls*, *Rocking Horse Hill*, *Heartland*, *Heart of the Valley*, *Promises* and *The French Prize*.

CHAPTER ONE

Harry Argyle never saw the horse. Not fully. He saw something with a huge black arse and, knowing that hitting things with big arses never turned out pretty, he swerved. A sideways skid and spray of gravel later and his ute was nose down in the overgrown gutter that ran alongside Redbank Road – the one the district council never mowed or repaired no matter how many times he complained – and repeating a word that'd earn him a solid clip over the ear from his mum, should she hear it.

He swore again to dispel the last traces of his shock and jammed the ute into reverse, easing it out of the gutter and back onto the unsealed road. Fat arse had turned around and now stood blinking at the headlights and puffing steam into the cold night, and regarding Harry as if he was the anomaly in this scene.

"A horse. Jesus." He scratched his head and stared at it.

The dumb thing took a step forward, its fine ears at attention. He could see now that its coat wasn't black but a rich dark brown. A white star shone in the middle of its forehead.

"To line up where the bullet goes," muttered

Harry, although he didn't mean it. He liked horses. They reminded him a bit of himself: not the smartest animals in the world, but big, brown-eyed, friendly, and kind of sweet.

He changed into neutral and left the car to idle. Outside the warm interior the night had chilled considerably. Sign of another fine one tomorrow. It was almost November and so far spring in this lower south-eastern corner of South Australia had been perfect. Periodic soaking rains followed by sunshiny days that stimulated the pasture and left his family's stud Simmentals grazing in lush, knee-high grass.

The horse whickered a soft equine hello and took a step forward. Harry scanned the road, checking for other cars. The moon was a thin crescent, the southern constellations bright, the night inky. Only his headlights lit the narrow country road. Redbank Road tended to be the reserve of local property owners and the occasional hoon looking for a patch of gravel on which to practice being a dickhead, but even they'd been put off by the potholes that pockmarked the surface, thanks to a wet winter. Harry used it on his trips into town from the farm because he liked the quiet, plus it took him past Maya Higgins's house, allowing him to wistfully wonder what she was dreaming about in her bed. Wishing it was him.

The horse took another couple of steps toward him. Harry walked closer and held out his hand for the horse to sniff, then stroked its nose, smiling in spite of himself. From its docility he figured it was someone's riding horse. He scanned its body as best as he could in the headlights. Frowning, he crouched to inspect the animal's forelegs closer. The horse sniffed and nuzzled Harry's hair as he reached out to trace the cut marks. They didn't look too bad, superficial scratches from barbed wire probably. He glanced across the road toward old Gav's farm. Gav was a drunken no-hoper who did nothing to upkeep the property he'd inherited by default from his uncle thirty years before. Every time Harry looked at the place he seethed at the waste.

He rose and with another light pat of the horse headed back to the ute for a torch, wishing Lucy was in the back so he could let her off to go sniffing. But his kelpie was at home with the other dogs, sleeping off a day's activity.

He directed the torchlight across the road and studied the fence line, searching for a breach. Even in the darkness the shocking state of Gav's farm was obvious. So sagged were some of the wires that the animal could have crossed at any number of places. He eyed the horse again and shone the torch over its flanks. Could be a jumper given its build, not that the fence would pose much of a challenge, especially for a horse with a hankering for green feed. Something Gav's place lacked badly.

Harry swept the light across the other side of the road just to make sure. He needn't have bothered. That land belonged to the Davidsons and they were pretty smart operators. Their twin girls were toddlers, not even at the pony-riding stage, and Harry doubted they'd offer horse agistment, whereas old Gav would chase every cent he could get. Plus Harry thought he'd seen the horse before when he'd passed. Just a glimpse of its hindquarters as it ambled over the hill, but definitely at Gav's.

With a sigh he turned off the torch and dumped it on the ute's bonnet before unbuckling his belt and threading it out of the loops of his jeans. He circled the leather around the horse's neck, making a clicking noise with his tongue as he tugged. After a yearning glance toward the opposite paddock, the horse dropped his head in resignation and followed like a dopey puppy.

Away from the headlights, Harry waited for his eyes to adjust to the night. On Gav's side of the road the grass was tall and rank; great tussocks of phalaris and Victoria ryegrass mixed with swathes of bracken that hadn't seen a slasher in years. The horse trailed him along the road edge, a great amiable bulk of warmth at Harry's shoulder. At the far end of the paddock a fencepost listed heavily outwards, its base almost rotted through, its collapse prevented only by three strands of loose barbed wire. The horse wouldn't have even needed to jump. A couple of steps would have done it, although one misstep and it could have knotted itself in a disastrous tangle.

Harry stood studying the fence, the horse calmly by his side as though in shared contemplation. This needed more tools than he had at hand, but he could manage enough of a running repair to keep the animal safe at least for the night. Releasing another disgruntled huff, he led the horse back to the gate and through, unwrapped his belt, and gave its silky coat another pat. He watched it for a moment as it shook its head and ambled away, sniffing the ground, then he latched the gate and headed back to the ute.

Harry had pliers and baling twine and not much else, but if he could tighten the wires enough, maybe string a bit of orange twine, it'd at least hold the post up. The horse hung close as he worked, its eyes catching the shine of the moon, strangely comforting. Satisfied he'd done all he could, Harry gave the horse a last nose rub, cast a filthy look toward the farmhouse, and strode back to his car.

"For fuck's sake!"

Harry slammed the brakes of his ute as once again the tyres skidded on the gravel. At least today the horse wasn't on the road. He stood at the edge, oblivious, happily tucking into a patch of purple flowering lucerne. Not that it needed the extra feed. Clearly someone was looking after it – a horse couldn't get that fit and sleek on Gav's pastures alone.

Good thing Harry had decent tools in the tray, not that he should have to repair Gav's bloody fence anyway. That was the landowner's responsibility, but relying on the old drunk was a waste of time. Something the horse's owner should surely know by now. Cattle and sheep could be problems enough, but horses, with their flighty, dumb natures, could cause all sorts of havoc. What if it'd been hoons driving along the road, or a young mum distracted by her children? Or Maya? Could've been a disaster.

The thought made Harry fume. It pissed him off mightily that people could be so irresponsible. Whoever owned this animal needed a good kick up the arse, and when Harry found out who it was he planned to let rip.

He spent half an hour going over the roadside fence, cursing for most of it, and wondering why he was wasting his time. But if he didn't do it he suspected it simply wouldn't get done, and it wasn't the horse's fault. He'd hate to see the animal hurt because he was too absorbed in his own grumpiness to do the right thing.

Satisfied, he headed to Gav's place, determined to take his mood out on someone.

The old man took his time answering. Noises echoed within. Muttered curses and things being knocked. The door opened a crack, emitting a disgusting whiff of sweat and alcohol tinged with a sour undercurrent of urine. Another blast of fury at the horse owner thundered through Harry. It was probably the agistment fees that were keeping Gav in booze.

"Yeah?"

"Who owns the horse, Gav?"

The old man rubbed his eyes, his raised arm releasing a waft of body odour. "Young girl. Why?"

"Because the bloody thing keeps getting out.

Twice this week."

Gav looked at him as if to say "So?"

"You need to fix that fence. With the road the way it is someone could get killed."

"I'll get onto it," said Gav in a way that revealed he'd heard all this before and knew what answer to give, but his weary, couldn't-give-a-rat's-arse tone shone through.

"When?" Harry persisted.

"Next couple of days."

He began to push the door shut. Harry stuck his size thirteen foot against it. "Make sure you do."

"Yeah, yeah."

"I'll be back to check."

Gav's gaze, until now rheumy and uncaring, developed a touch of steel. Harry matched it with an expression equally as tough, and from a bloke who stood a shade short of two metres tall and weighed over a hundred kilos, tough had serious meaning. Gav looked away first.

Message delivered, Harry removed his boot. The door slammed shut immediately. He took a few steps away and inhaled, grateful for the fresh air.

What made a man get like that?

He shook his head. How the old soak treated himself was no business of his, but the moment he put others in danger, especially people Harry cared about, that was a different matter. Maya used this road. If anything happened to her he'd never forgive himself.

*

Summer Taylor checked the fence with delight. Her desperate entreaties to Gav must have finally triggered the man to action. Although makeshift, all the top strands of the fence were in place, while the rotting post that keep toppling over was fixed upright, thanks to a well-hammered star dropper and a base packed tight with soil. Not perfect by any means, but enough to keep Binky where he belonged.

With her horse tied securely to the gnarly old pine she used as a makeshift hitching rail, Summer opened the gate and drove into the paddock, smiling with affection at Binky as he stared longingly toward his escape route. The greedy guts could sniff lucerne from a mile off and the horse was forever trying to sneak through the gate to get to the volunteer plants that sprouted along the opposite verge of the road.

She parked her SUV on the safe side of Gav's hay shed. The posts holding it up listed westward so alarmingly that Summer was always surprised to find it still standing. It was dangerous, but the only shelter available to store Binky's hard feed. His precious bales of hay she kept under a heavy tarpaulin in front, with a double-stranded electric fence surrounding the lot. For a while she'd contemplated using large concrete pavers to keep the tarp in place, and moving the electric fence to the paddock's front boundary, but experience had taught her Binky was an expert at finding ways into feed, no matter how well covered. With premium lucerne going for well over ten dollars a bale, hay was too expensive to squander and money was tight. Feeding Binky was costing her a small fortune as it was and Summer couldn't afford any wastage.

Binky stamped and shuffled as she fetched a casserole dish off the car's rear seat. Backing out, Summer blew kisses his way. "Patience, baby." A bump of her hip shut the car door and with a duck through another loosely wired fence, she carried the casserole toward Gav's house.

A chook shot off into the backyard's long grass, squawking. Hidden beneath an unclipped box hedge, a calico cat lurked, attention tuned for birds. Summer hissed, scaring the cat off, and made a mental reminder to find a collar with a bell for it.

She knocked and called out, waiting a moment before pushing the door open a sliver. "Gav? It's Summer."

Creaks sounded from further in the house. She sniffed cautiously, wondering how bad it would be, but the air was free of the rank stench of vomit that had been there two days prior. Anguish rose in her chest. He'd probably run out of money to pay for booze, and now she was going to hand over her agistment fee.

Except what was she meant to do? She couldn't not pay him. Nor was she responsible for Gav's alcoholism. With limited resources, all Summer could do was show some human kindness. Although that didn't make it easier to bear. Or remove the guilt.

"Gav, I'm coming in. I've brought you chicken and veg pie. I'll just put it in the oven to heat, okay?"

She pushed the door open wider and surveyed the kitchen. Dishes lined the sink. A couple of empty mugs were on the kitchen table, the local *Levenham Leader* newspaper nearby. Clean, by Gav's standards.

In the background she could hear the faint trickle of water. Summer headed for the oven and cranked it on before sliding the foil-covered casserole inside. By the time she'd finished with Binky, Gav's meal would be ready and she'd have a few minutes to chat and ensure he would receive at least some decent nutrition.

Everything set, she slipped back outside.

Binky stood stoically under the tree as she saddled him. The early evening was hushed, almost lonely sounding, and not for the first time Summer wished for home. For the landscape she'd grown up with, her friends, her mum and dad and two brothers. The safety of familiarity. But unless she wanted to continue the rest of her life unemployed and sponging off her parents, or stuck doing a job she hated, Levenham would have to do. It wasn't perfect but she'd scored a good position with a reputable business and, compared to the last disaster, that was a major plus.

Binky nudged her shoulder as she tapped the top of his off foreleg. She lifted it up and drew it gently toward her, stretching and smoothing the skin beneath the saddle's girth. After repeating the same exercise with his nearside leg, she gave him a last pat, put her foot in the stirrup, and vaulted lightly into the saddle.

Sunset was already drifting in, dappling the paddocks in peach and saffron, and granting Gav's bracken-infested pastures a strange dusky prettiness. Summer would have preferred to take Binky for a long walk around the roads, get him away from the boredom of the farm, but her last client had arrived late and then a staff meeting had delayed her further.

She urged Binky into his silky trot. It was the beautiful dark bay coat that seemed to shimmer when he moved that had first attracted Summer to him, but it was the sheer elegance of his paces that sealed the deal – a beautiful floaty trot that made Binky look like he was walking on air. In extended trot he seemed to skate, as if the ground was made of ice and he was surging across it in sweeps.

Beyond Gav's boundary the surrounding lush paddocks were vivid in the failing light, their plants filling the air with a delicious herbaceous scent. Lucerne ready for cutting. Nitrogen-fixing white clover bright against the limier grasses. Shiny-leafed ryegrass. Duller fescue and cocksfoot. Gav's farm was like a crooked, ragged patch in an otherwise beautifully crafted quilt.

Summer exercised Binky near the rear fence, on the paddock's single strip of flat ground, practicing shoulder-ins, counter-canters and tight, ten metre circles, his snorts echoing in the country quiet. There wasn't a lot to like about Gav's farm but she appreciated its relative isolation and stillness. This felt peaceful and private, as if she and Binky were the only domesticated creatures left on earth. And it was a pleasant way to end a busy day.

The bracken was glowing a sickly hazel in the sun's last light when Summer ended her ride. She patted Binky's neck and walked him back to the hayshed, wondering if she could ask Gav to slash the paddock. She hoped her horse possessed enough nous not to eat the fern fronds, but with the other vegetation so poor there was a chance he might. A little was harmless, but too much could lead to thiamine deficiency and Binky staggering around like a drunk at a Bachelor and Spinster's Ball.

Summer dismounted and ran her hands over his coat, assessing his well-filled belly and rump. He seemed healthy enough but that would never stop her worrying. After unsaddling and brushing Binky down, she drew back the tarp protecting her stash of feed. The horse's nostrils flared and his dark brown eyes took on that pleading look she knew so well and adored, an almost childlike entreaty for "more, please". Summer levered off a couple of biscuits of lucerne hay and tossed them into a low rubber feed tub. Binky greedily tucked in, leaving her free to mix up his hard feed in another, smaller tub.

She placed the bucket alongside his hay and watched, amused, as Binky plunged his nose inside and closed his eyes in ecstasy. She scrubbed his mane as he munched, chattering affectionate nonsense, before returning to secure the feed and reactivate the electric fence.

Chores done and her horse happy, she headed back to the house.

Gav was at the kitchen table, a mug by his hand. His hair was still a little damp, his usually bristled jaw smooth. A woodsy scent hung in the air from the cologne he'd obviously applied.

Summer smiled. "You're looking perky."

"Going out."

The envelope in her pocket dug its pointed corner into her hip. Summer bet he was. As soon as his fingers closed around her agistment money he'd be off. With effort, she kept the dismay from her face and headed for the oven.

"You don't have to cook for me. I can take care of myself."

"I told you, it's leftovers. This girl can't live on tofu. I need meat."

Gav grunted. "Should be able to eat what you want in your own house."

"True, but it's not that easy." As Summer had discovered, much to her chagrin.

The last time Summer had brought home a thick rib steak for herself, on a night when her housemates Lissa and Lori were meant to be out, the girls had arrived home unexpectedly. A single glance at the table where the steak lay coming up to room temperature and Lissa had turned pale. Lori had clapped her hand over her mouth in horror before turning her angry gaze on Summer. If they hadn't been so desperate to share the rent on their big old house, Summer would have been out on her ear, regardless of the agreement they'd supposedly established before she'd moved in. Rental accommodation-seeking vegetarians were hard to come by in Levenham and circumstances meant they'd been forced to loosen their housemate criteria. Summer was allowed to cook meat whenever the girls were out, as long as she cleaned up and aired the place appropriately afterward. That they'd arrived home early was hardly her fault, but that hadn't stopped Lissa and Lori acting as though it was.

To keep the peace, Summer cooked herself pastas and stir-fries, and occasionally shared a meal with the others. Some were awful, others surprisingly tasty, but eventually her craving for meat would become too much. On those occasions, she'd cook enough for several helpings, stowing leftovers in plastic containers in the freezer, wrapped in foil to hide the contents from Lissa and Lori's delicate eyes. When Summer had started bringing Gav meals it was as much for her sake as his. She enjoyed a serve of protein without fear of offence, and Gav gained some much-needed nutrition.

She used tea towels to hold the hot casserole and carried it to the sink drainer. Enticing smells teased her nostrils and caused her stomach to rumble. Gav fetched plates for her and laid out cutlery and placemats on the table, adding salt, pepper and a bottle of tomato sauce to the centre.

Summer tried not to cringe at the sauce, but Gav had it with everything, as if that was the only flavour he could tolerate. Perhaps it was more to cover up the taste of vegetables. Or that his tastebuds had been desensitised by alcohol. Either way it didn't matter. He was eating, and that's what counted.

They sat down to their meal, neither feeling the need to talk. Summer had found the quiet disconcerting at first. Dinner at her parents' was always raucous, full of news and local gossip, mixed with the occasional good-hearted ribbing about Summer or her brothers' love lives. Or lack thereof in Summer's case. With Lissa and Lori, conversation was skewed mainly to politics, which her housemates adored and had strong opinions about, often in conflict with Summer's more conservative leanings. But she enjoyed the debate and was open-minded enough to appreciate a point well made.

With Gav it was the clink of cutlery, the occasional mutter about the weather or the local council, and the creak of the old house.

"You go," he said when they'd finished. "I'll wash up."

"No, I'll help. I want to take the dish home with me anyway."

She didn't need it. All she wanted was to delay his trip into the bottle shop for a little longer. She hadn't handed over her month's agistment money yet, though she'd caught Gav glancing at her pocket in expectation.

He washed fast, scrubbing with nervous energy, his desire oozing out of him the way alcohol would from his pores in the morning. Summer knew that smell too well – the stench of hopelessness and self-hatred. It had cost her grandfather his life.

Finally, when she could delay no longer, she pulled the envelope from her pocket and laid it on the table. She cast Gav a pleading look, but he was already slipping on a jacket and fetching the keys to his ute.

He caught her gaze and looked away, toward an old polished buffet and hutch and the gold-framed wedding portrait it held. His mouth worked for a moment, his eyes glazing, then he stared at the floor before looking up, not quite making eye contact.

"I'll see you tomorrow then."

"Sure," replied Summer. On impulse she stretched up and kissed Gav on the cheek, taking him by surprise.

"What was that for?"

"For fixing the front fence."

Bottom lip sucked in, he glanced aside again, crunching his keys in his fist. "Wouldn't want Binky getting hurt."

"No."

She patted his arm and opened the back door. Dark rambled, thick and ominous, causing a small shudder to course through her. Summer checked back over her shoulder, her voice soft. "Be careful, Gav."

Shame kept his head lowered.

Summer had barely reached the paddock gate when Gav reversed his ute out onto the road. She swung the gate open and turned her back as dismay yanked her insides. Thanks to her, Gav was about to destroy more of his body, not to mention his state of mind. She trudged back to the car, reminding herself that this wasn't her fault. That Gav wasn't her responsibility. He wasn't grandpa.

She slumped heavily in the driver's seat and put the SUV into gear, only for her dismay to worsen the moment she looked up.

"Binky!"

Taking advantage of her distraction, Binky was sauntering happily through the gate, his one-track mind intent on the lucerne growing so lushly on the other side of the road. Usually he could be relied on to stay by his feed buckets, but tonight his hunger for decent green feed proved too overwhelming.

Putting the car back into neutral, Summer snatched a lead rope off the back seat, alighted and strode after him, calling out. Usually he was easy to catch, but Binky appeared to be in one of his moods, and intent on playing funny buggers. Ignoring her, he tossed his head and broke into a trot.

Just as another car appeared through the dust left in Gav's wake.

"Binky!"

The driver braked hard. Gravel spewed from behind the vehicle's locked up wheels but the skid was flinging the car closer and closer to Binky.

Panicked, Summer ran after her horse, waving her arms in an attempt to scare him into a bolt. Anything to chase him out of danger. A horn blasted the night. The four-wheel drive veered, turned sideways on the road and spun, its massive bullbar just missing Summer's leg. Terror-stricken, she slipped on the loose stones and fell heavily onto her hands and knees.

The engine cut. A dust cloud hung. Then someone was running.

"Jesus Christ, are you all right?"

Summer looked up to find a giant standing over her. "Yes." She took a shuddery breath and assessed herself. Her heart was racketing painfully around her chest and her hands and knees throbbed. "Yes, I'm fine. Thanks."

The giant bent down and touched her elbow. "Here, let me help you up."

She squinted. With the car headlights behind him she couldn't see his face, only that he had short hair and slightly protruding ears. His voice was nice though, deep and masculine.

"It's okay. I can manage." Breathing hard, she stood and checked her grazed hands, then tested a couple of steps. Her skin and bruised knees hurt like blazes but her injuries were minor. She winced a reassuring smile. "I'm not hurt." And right now she was more worried about Binky.

Summer limped toward him. The animal seemed oblivious to the drama it had caused. He raised his head at her approach, stems of lucerne disappearing inside his rapidly chewing mouth.

"This is your horse?" asked the giant.

"Yes." She patted Binky's neck while checking him over. Not a scratch. Typical. "I'm really sorry about this."

"Sorry? *Sorry*? What the fuck?"

Summer's eyes widened. Alarmed by the

aggression in his tone and aware she was alone on a dark country road with a man twice her size, she braced herself and faced him fully. The dust was beginning to settle, eerie in the twilight. The light behind showed off the man's enormous silhouette; hands on his head, elbows wide, legs apart. No longer solicitous. Menacing.

Summer dug her fingers into a hunk of Binky's mane, watching warily.

He began to pace back and forth in front of the headlights, like a creepy character out of one of those lonely road urban legends. "You could have killed someone!"

"I'm sorry."

Suddenly he whirled around and strode toward her, finger jabbing. "This is the third fucking time! Sorry isn't good enough."

Her grip on Binky's mane tensed. Summer tried not to cringe at his proximity, at the fierceness of his body language and tone, even though her heart was jack-hammering and her own vulnerability was rapidly closing around her like a fist. She could see his features now. He was around her age perhaps, but with an old-fashioned look about him, thanks to his traditional haircut and prominent ears. But it was his fury that was terrifying.

"It was an accident."

He stared at her like she was an idiot. "The first time might have been an accident. The second was carelessness, but this," – he flung a hand toward Binky – "this is beyond irresponsibility. And what the fuck were you doing running after the stupid animal like that? I was this close" – he pinched his thumb and forefinger together – "to killing you!"

"I didn't think."

"That much is frigging obvious." He scanned her up and down, mouth curling slightly at the sight of her tight breeches, half-chaps and boots, before returning his contemptuous glare to hers. "Looks to me like you don't think too much about anything."

Tears began to prickle Summer's eyes but she was stuffed if she was going to show her distress in front of this pig of a man. Who did he think he was? It was an accident!

The apish bully directed a pointed finger at the paddock. "Look at that fence. You haven't even touched it."

"Gav said he'd get onto it. He's already made a few repairs."

The man let out a savage bark of laughter that carried no amusement at all. "Gav? That old drunk? He can't even thread his own belt." He took a step closer to Summer, his Olympic swimmer-sized shoulders cutting off the headlights' glow, leaving only emerging moonlight. Glittering eyes bored into hers. "Get that fence fixed before you kill someone."

Biting the inside of her lip, Summer held his gaze, her back straight. She forced her voice strong. "I'm sorry. It won't happen again."

"It had better not."

And with a final mean glare at her and Binky, he stomped back to his ute.

To discover more about *Summer and the Groomsman* and my other books, please visit cathrynhein.com or your favourite bookseller.